Simon Raven was born in  Charterhouse and King's Co Classics. Afterwards he served Infantry. In 1957 he resigned book reviewing. His first novel, *The Feathers of Death*, brought instant recognition and his popular *First-Born of Egypt* series encompasses seven volumes. His TV and radio plays, of which *Royal Foundation* is the best known, are classics. He also wrote the scripts for the *Pallisers* series and *Edward and Mrs Simpson*.

SIMON RAVEN

Bird of Ill Omen

HOUSE OF
STRATUS

This edition published in 2001 by House of Stratus, an imprint of
Stratus Holdings plc, 24c Old Burlington Street, London, W1X 1RL, UK.

www.houseofstratus.com

Typeset, printed and bound by House of Stratus.

A catalogue record for this book is available from the British Library.

ISBN 1-84232-174-9

Contents

PREFACE

This is a book of journeys, all of which have one thing in common, that they ended in mishap, in some cases in grave disaster, to one or more of the travellers. These mishaps and disasters, in their turn, also have one thing in common: that they were, to some extent, caused, provoked, initiated, or at any rate made possible, by myself. In no case did I bear malice or make plots; so far from intending evil I wished for everyone concerned everything he would have wished for himself; had I known even of the barest likelihood of the misfortunes which I am about to relate I should have done everything I conceivably could to prevent them. And yet…all of them somehow originated, had their prime movement, in some act of my own – sometimes an act that took place many thousands of miles from the calamity itself, many days, weeks or even months before this calamity occurred. Something which I had done or said or ordered or suggested, some utterly casual remark, some extra but (as I thought) necessary chore or precaution, some minor protest against trivial injustice or some modest effort to correct misunderstanding – something of my saying or making had set in train a series of events which ended in sorrow or catastrophe.

These actions or impulses of mine, which were to have such disagreeable or even hideous results, were seldom culpable in themselves or in relation to their circumstances, were indeed sometimes intelligent or virtuous. Even when ill considered or

i

self-indulgent, they certainly did not deserve to issue in misery or bloodshed. I cannot stress too much that they were ordinary, everyday proceedings, often so slight that they were forgotten the next moment and only recalled when the thread that connected them to subsequent and consequent disaster later and with hindsight became visible. There is, I perceive, nothing we do in this world, however slight, of which we may not, in the future near or far, and after unforeseen and ineluctable processes of time and chance, be called to render account.

Sometimes the accounting must be public, if the connection between cause and effect be plain to all; more often, in the intricate and elusive nature of most of these cases, this connection is known only to a very few people (perhaps only to one) who have good reason to hold their peace. In the former type of instance, the *actum* or *dictum* that started it all off will sometimes be seen as a deliberate attempt to make trouble, though it will seldom have operated in the precise manner or direction intended. In this book, on the other hand, I am concerned with *acta* or *dicta* that were intended to achieve nothing beyond some minor and beneficent local effect – were intended, often enough, merely to amuse or to illustrate. So in the following pages, there can be neither blame nor accusation, as regards myself or anyone else. One may, however, observe a pattern. Even the most innocent comment made in the course of everyday affairs will probably refer to flaws or foibles (however trifling) and even the most temperate exercise in directing or tidying will presuppose something to be directed or tidied. Error, when corrected, is often the more remarkable for this attention; and if it is the more remarkable it is the more remarked, often assuming an importance which it could never have had while merely overlooked. The same can be said of folly as of error. Once either of them has been pointed out, people are thereafter concerned to look for more of it, if it be that of others, and to disown, excuse or justify it if it be their own. Thus a new and often very dangerous element is introduced into affairs: a new force has been (albeit unintentionally) conjured and may happen blindly on devious passages to vulnerable posterns, causing bloody alarum and excursion.

It is this process – the awakening of dormant disaster which may be brought about by any human act or speech, no matter how casual or innocent – that I am to illustrate here in this book of journeys. Of course I am not saying that everything we do or say will eventually result in catastrophe, but only that comment and correction are particularly likely to cause unhappy vibrations that may irritate the very lesions which one aims to cure. There is nothing to be done about any of this, no way of ensuring that one is never the cause (however inadvertent) of misfortune, other than by lying in bed gagged for one's entire life. Not a practicable scheme. In any case, as I shall show, the whole thing, in the end, is simply a matter of luck. You may shoot your mouth off like Big Bertha all your life and never cause a single tear to flow; or you may make one jolly little joke about tennis balls and massacre the chivalry of France.

PART ONE

Deolali Tap
or
The Devil's Cadet

In the autumn of 1946, His Majesty's Troopship *Georgic* sailed from Liverpool bound for Bombay and carrying thousands of disgruntled soldiers of all ranks, 300 of them, rather more attractive than the rest, being officer cadets of infantry, among these Jerry Constant Stanley and myself. We were all to attend the officers' training school at Bangalore in the state of Mysore (South India) because there were not enough officer cadet training units in Britain. Thank God there weren't, we said to one another: British OCTUs were dank, dull and ferocious, with a failure rate of twenty-eight per cent; in Bangalore (or so the rumour went) you could not fail, so much money had been spent on transporting you there, unless you died, went mad, or got the pox – three times at that. This rumour, it should be said, was pretty near true, but not quite, a qualification which may be remembered later in this story. By the end of 1946, of course, it was much too late to turn us out as officers of the Indian Army, which henceforth (and God help it, we all said) would be officered by Indians; all of us would be commissioned into British regiments of the line and distributed round the many British battalions still in India or the Far East. More of this intention presently; just now, back to the 300 cadets and in particular to Jerry Stanley, a tall, clean, amiable, well-mannered cadet, rather weak-minded and pampered (too pretty for his own good), conceited when sober, loud and fatuous when in his not infrequent cups.

Jerry's failings, like those of the rest of us, were not diminished by the easy circumstances and indulgent treatment which we enjoyed on HMT *Georgic* and later in a Transit Camp called Khalyan, near Bombay. We were paid as serjeants, addressed as 'Sir', and waited upon, as soon as we reached India, by one quarter of a native bearer or servant per cadet. Even as early as Khalyan, a good month before we reached the OTS at Bangalore, the characters of all of us had deteriorated, and nobody's so conspicuously and, in a way, so attractively, as that of Jerry Stanley.

'Jerry Stanley is the Devil's Cadet,' my old school chum, James Prior, used to say.

'Have you heard what he's done now?' said a budding Morgan Grenfell. 'He took a day's leave in Bombay, found himself without money, marched into Barclays DCO and asked to see the manager. And they let him. It was his riding whip which did the trick – he carried it with such *panache*.'

'No officer in the infantry under field rank, unless he holds a mounted appointment such as that of adjutant, is allowed to carry a riding whip,' said puffy, pedantic Giles Benson.

'Jerry Stanley was carrying his like a colonel of cavalry,' said Morgan Grenfell. 'He looked so splendid, I'm told, that we might even have let him into one of *our* banks. But I don't think we should have let him have any money – which the manager of this branch of Barclays DCO was silly enough to do. Jerry said there was a draft on the way for his credit with Barclays DCO in Bangalore, so could he have some cash *here*, the sum to be debited to his account *there*. The manager nearly melted under Jerry's gaze, lent him twice as much as he first asked for – twenty pounds' worth of rupees – and was rewarded with a stylish flourish of the whip and a magnificent salute. But this morning the bank manager in Bombay telephoned the Commandant here and Jerry was summoned. It seemed that his account in Bangalore was a complete invention, and as for the draft – mere fantasy. Like Billy Bunter's postal order.'

'Disgraceful,' pouted Giles.

'How did Jerry get out of it?' I said. 'I've just seen him, large as a lion, piping up a huge round of gins in the cadets' mess.'

'He said,' said Morgan Grenfell, 'that it was all an unfortunate mistake. The branch of Barclays which his family used in England had either misunderstood or mismanaged his father's instructions. And of course the expense and bother of checking this with England were so enormous, and Jerry's face was so innocent, and his uniform so crisp, and his manner so pleasant and tactful (no riding whip today, of course, only a modest cadet's split cane), that the Commandant was only too happy to accept Jerry's explanation and order that the money should be paid to the manager in Bombay and debited to Jerry's account with the army paymaster. Not a single hard word – and Jerry invited to curry tiffin on Sunday with the Commandant and what's left of his wife. He'll be moving into the Commandant's quarter before you can say *burra peg*.'

'Where did he get the cash to pay for all those gins in the mess?' said Giles peevishly. (Even in the Indian transit camps they weren't so absurd as to give the cadets drink on credit.)

'He asked me for a small loan,' giggled the scion of the House of Morgan Grenfell. 'I hadn't the heart to say "no".'

'The Devil's Cadet,' mused Jim Prior with a grin that ran the entire width of his huge moon face. 'God be praised for the variety of His creatures.'

A little later came the row about Jerry's performance on the fairground. Like all garrison towns in India at that time, Khalyan had a fair which it was hoped (absolutely in vain) would divert the soldiery from the native bawds. The two main attractions in this fair were the 'divebomber', when not out of order, and the 'wall of death', when the death rider was sober enough to mount his motorcycle. On one occasion when he was not, Jerry, who understood the anti-gravity principle of this simple proceeding, volunteered to take his part. After a brief period of practice, he was pronounced competent and rode to several audiences with some distinction. All of which might have been well enough, had he not, at the conclusion of his last performance, taken the motorcycle as well as his pay and driven off into the native bazaar (as opposed to the military one).

'And what did he do then?' enquired James Prior placidly.

'No one knows. Though most have been uncharitable.'

'The native bazaar is out of bounds,' announced Giles Benson vengefully, 'as Stanley very well knew. The penalty is to be deprived of his cadetship and sent home – or to some British unit in India – as a private.'

'Oh dear, no,' said Morgan Grenfell. 'The authorities wouldn't like that after taking such trouble to get him here. They'd say that Jerry hadn't been properly looked after. So the Commandant has been easily persuaded that Jerry's brain had been confused by the prolonged gyration, and that all he meant to do was to ride the bike to its shed and park it there for the night, but somehow he lost control.'

'He had no business performing on the fairground anyway,' said Giles.

'Oh?' said James. 'And would you ride the wall of death?'

'It's just a trick; everyone knows that.'

'Not a trick I'd care to try,' said James.

'That was what the Commandant said,' said Morgan Grenfell. ' "Bravo, my boy," said the Commandant. "But please, Mr Stanley, let us have no more controversial goings-on between now and when you leave for Bangalore. Dinner on Friday? My wife would like to say goodbye to you." '

'What it is to have favour,' sighed 'Lusto' Lovibond, our platoon melancholic.

'Luck, I think, in this case,' said James. 'Lucky soldiers should always be indulged; they're much too useful to lose.'

'That's what Napoleon thought,' said Morgan Grenfell. 'He made them marshals of France.'

'The first step is to become a second lieutenant,' said Giles. 'As to that, we'll see.'

In the event, Jerry got clear of Khalyan without any more 'controversial goings-on' – unless you count being carried on to the train by loyal fellow cadets after a farewell overdose of Parry's Military Rum.

'It will be interesting to see what happens to Jerry in Bangalore,' said James, 'when he's had time to settle in and take a good look at the wicket. I always felt that his scope has been far too confined in Khalyan – that he didn't, so to speak, have "World enough and time".'

The first person Jerry saw in Bangalore, almost the moment he got off the train, was the prefect for whom he had fagged at Cranford five years previously.

Bruce Brewster had not prospered in the army. This was not for want of trying, nor even for want of ability (at that time exceedingly little was required); it was simply because he possessed not one amiable quality. Nor, for that matter, did he have any notably unpleasant qualities either. He was not odious; he was, so to speak, nullity – nullity on two stout legs, nullity with a quacking voice but one quite adequate to marshal soldiers on a parade ground or bring them up to attention on the arrival of the officer who was to address them about team spirit or tropical disease.

Obsessively clean, Serjeant Brewster always looked slightly dirty; he did not smell, but smelt so officiously of nothing (almost as though he had a neutral zone round his entire body) that one would much have preferred a little warm, human BO. He was of an intelligence so precisely average, so mathematically medial, that, while he seldom erred, he neither initiated nor achieved. He could instruct but not teach; walk in front but not lead; issue orders but not command. A decent and conscientious man, he made his superiors feel so guilty by his virtuous presence that they longed for his absence and as soon as he was out of the room forgot him absolutely – or rather, remembered him with mild uneasiness for just long enough to arrange for him to be posted elsewhere; but never where he wished to be posted – to an OCTU or an OTS as an officer cadet. He fought his way through, by sheer persistence, to selection board after selection board, but none would pass him; each one just passed him over or at best on to another.

Brewster was pleased to see Jerry and shook him by the hand on the platform.

'I've been looking forward to this,' Brewster said. 'I saw from the roll that you were coming and as luck will have it you'll be under me for weapon training.'

He looked at Officer Cadet Stanley, who looked back at Serjeant Brewster.

'But not for long, I think,' Brewster went on, truthful, earnest, without forwardness or conceit. 'I'm to have another board at the end of the month. I'm hoping they'll send me to the OTS at Quetta – this one would be out, of course, as I've been training cadets here – or even to receive an immediate commission in recognition of my long service in the ranks.' He did not attempt to explain or excuse this. 'But that's not till the end of the month,' he said. 'We'll be seeing a bit of one another until then.'

Questioned, later, about what sort of fag-master Brewster had been, Jerry was loyal but vague.

'I can't seem to remember anything about him,' Jerry said. 'He never beat me, I do remember that. In fact it's what he *didn't* do that is clearest. You know, I don't think he actually *did* anything at all. Oh yes: he insisted on a decent shine on his shoes.'

Further enquiry elicited, after long pauses for thought by Jerry, that Brewster had been in the 3rd XI at cricket, the Under VIth for science and had become a house prefect (never a school one) because his record was so blameless that it was impossible to neglect his claim (however negative) any longer.

'A good man,' said Jerry dubiously. 'Rather embarrassing all this – I mean, me being a cadet and him just a serjeant. I must say, he doesn't seem to bear a grudge or anything like that.'

Nor did he. On parade he treated Jerry like any other cadet, i.e. dully but correctly. Off parade they occasionally had a meal together at Ley Wong's Chinese restaurant, until Brewster announced, to Jerry's politely concealed relief, that the RSM had counselled him that it was ill-advised for instructors to consort with cadets, whatever their former relation.

'So this is our last little forgathering,' said Bruce Brewster. 'Anyway, I hope I shan't be here much longer. In three days I'm off for my board and I rather expect' – this with entire lack of velleity or presumption – 'that they'll be arranging something else for me.'

So off went Brewster for his board in Mysore, which was to take ten days. Normal boards took only three. The official explanation of this expansion in the case of Serjeant Brewster was that since he was being considered for an immediate commission more complicated analysis than usual would be required.

'Or that's what he told me,' said Jerry. 'Ten days. It's nice to have poor old Bruce out of the way for a bit. His presence was – well – rather repressive: it made me feel as if I was still a study fag and had better behave or else… Now,' he said with a spirited glint, 'I can be myself.'

And he went that very night to the Soldiers Three Tavern (a place of entertainment for Other Ranks only and so barred to cadets), where he picked up a chi-chi girl (our regrettable expression, in those days, for an Anglo-Indian in the sense of Eurasian).

'She's called Rosalie,' said Jerry. 'She's a stunner.'

'How much?' said Barry Barnes (a notable boxer).

'Nothing like that about Rosalie. She thinks I'm going to marry her and take her home with me. She calls England "home", you know – all these half-caste girls do, because their fathers were mostly Englishmen or Scotsmen in the railways. It's rather touching.'

'It'll be more than touching if she takes you at your word,' said Giles Benson.

'I didn't give my word. She thought the whole thing up herself.'

'Stay away from the Soldiers Three Tavern,' said James Prior.

'But I've promised Rosalie to meet her there tonight.'

'Then on your head be it,' said Giles.

'I hope,' said James, 'that you haven't given her your name.'

'Only Jerry.'

'Then keep the rest of it to yourself, if you don't want her mother up here, complaining to the Brigadier.'

'Right you be,' Jerry said.

So that night and many nights (so he informed us) Jerry held tryst with Rosalie, deserting her only once, to attend a celebration given by Bruce Brewster. For the board at Mysore had smiled upon Bruce at last and he had returned to Bangalore only to collect his stuff before proceeding to the OTS at Dehra Dun, where he was to attend a short course of six weeks for senior NCOs and warrant officers before becoming a full lieutenant.

'It couldn't have happened to a better man,' said Jerry luxuriantly to Bruce at Bruce's party and rendered the last verse of the Cranford School Song:

> '*Floreant Cranfordiani*
> *Qua sunt loci tropicani,*
> *Qua sunt milites Reginae,*
> *Quorum Enses et Vaginae*
>   *Procul lucent, procul vincunt,*
>   *Nunquam Ius et Fas relinquunt.*'

'*Vaginae?*' questioned James Prior.

'*Sheathes,*' said Bruce, a trifle crossly – 'Whose Swords and Sheathes shine afar, conquer afar, never desert the Just and the Right.'

'Bravo,' said James. 'That song might have been written for you.'

'Thank you,' said Bruce sincerely, without arrogance or false modesty. 'I do try, you know. The last three or four years have been very trying. Thank God it's all over now – Dehra Dun next week, then commissioned as lieutenant a few weeks later. I shall put myself up for a regular commission next summer or autumn. There's no life really like it.'

'Shush,' I said. 'Never let the gods know that you are happy. The gods, on the whole, are not in favour of human happiness.'

'*We* have a Christian God,' sniffed Giles.

'I dare say the same applies to Him,' remarked James; and shortly afterwards, after 'Three times three for Bruce Brewster' and 'He's a jolly good fellow', the party ended.

'Pity you can't behave with some of Bruce's responsibility,' said Giles to Jerry on the way back to our quarters.

'Bruce Brewster,' said Jerry, 'is the sort of chap that has his shower in his underpants in case someone else comes in and sees his cock. If that's being responsible, then you can keep it. And stuff it. But Bruce is a great chap and Cranford was a great school – '*Floreant Cranfordiani,*' he bawled, '*Qua sunt loci tropicani* – '

'Now, now,' said James. 'Most people are asleep and tomorrow will be a long day.'

It was. Even at Bangalore there was a pretence of work, reluctantly introduced out of respect for the war and still lingering. So the days were long, yet not really very arduous (as an elaborate but in part fictitious timetable allowed many plausible hiatuses and camouflaged much opportunity for lolling about), certainly not arduous enough to keep Jerry away from Rosalie.

At first no harm came of this: The days went placidly on. In place of Bruce Brewster we were given a mild, undemanding serjeant of fusiliers as an instructor in small arms. When the time came for the selection of cadet NCOs and under officers (about eight weeks after our arrival, with Christmas now long behind us) James Prior was appointed a junior under officer and therefore the leading man in our platoon, and Giles Benson was made a cadet serjeant. James wore his new rank lightly; Giles continued censorious, but though he now had official sanction to promulgate and enforce his judgments, he forbore, being a gentleman, to exact penalty and confined himself, like a Greek chorus, to moral complaint and foreboding.

'Jerry Stanley will come to no good,' he kept saying. 'That half-caste girl...'

'How often do I have to tell you,' said James, 'that Jerry is the Devil's Cadet? So he will be well taken care of. As for that girl, we only have his word for it that he is seeing her – indeed that she exists at all. He may be making the whole thing up to entertain us. He is very generous in that way.'

'He certainly goes to that tavern place,' said Giles, 'although it's out of bounds to cadets. I just happened to spot him as he went in there last Saturday.'

'Snooping, Giles?' I said.

'Don't worry. I shan't do anything about it. I just like to know what's going on, that's all.'

'But you don't,' said Barry the Boxer, 'know anything much at all. You didn't follow him in to check on that chi-chi girl? You didn't see him come out with her?'

'I've better things to do than hang around places like that. I came back to quarters to brush up on my military law and then went to bed.'

'So for all you know, it could be as James says? The girl may not even exist?'

But she existed all right. Oh dear, yes. And one day, Jerry told us, she announced (a) that she was pregnant and (b) that her old mother insisted on marriage.

Giles moaned and quivered, as if about to launch into a dithyramb of invective against human folly and lust.

'But she can't be pregnant,' Jerry insisted. 'I always used a thing.'

'They're not infallible,' said Morgan Grenfell. 'What are you going to do?'

'I've got a plan.'

'I yearn to hear it,' said James.

'Bruce Brewster is coming through in a day or two, *en route* for the Nilgeris. Lieutenant Bruce Brewster on his commissioning furlough. I'm going to give a little dinner party at Ley Wong's, to which I am now cordially inviting you all, get Bruce drunk (with your help) and afterwards introduce him to Rosalie. She will be impressed by a real officer – much swisher than a cadet. A full lieutenant at that. So I think I can simply leave the matter to her. Poor old Bruce is a bundle of frustrations and just now, flushed with success at last, he'll be off his guard.'

'But what on earth,' said Morgan Grenfell, 'do you think is going to happen?'

'God knows. But look at it like this. Bruce is a man totally without personality or attraction. In his whole life not a single woman, except possibly his mother, has even looked at him. Now if Rosalie takes an interest...encouraged by the thought that he's a millionaire...'

'You're going to lie to her?'

'Tit for tat. Anyway, Bruce could have become a millionaire for all I know. I remember, at school, hearing about some sort of uncle he had in the City. I shall simply pass that on to Rosalie. These girls are very greedy and very simple minded. They'll try anything on. Well, let her try something on Bruce.'

'Perfidy,' snorted Giles.

'Rather caddish, I must say,' said Morgan Grenfell.

'I don't know,' I contributed. 'Bruce may well get a bit of pleasure out of life at last.'

'And pay rather dear for it,' said James. 'Shall you ask Rosalie to the dinner?'

'No. I rely on you chaps to help me get Bruce nicely plastered and then I'll take him off to a special rendezvous.'

'Not at the Three Soldiers Tavern?'

'Bruce would never go into a place that was out of bounds, however drunk he was.'

'But he might let himself fall into the hands of Rosalie?'

'If given a little push…'

Jerry's dinner for Lieutenant Bruce Brewster got off to a bad start when Bruce revealed that during the course at Dehra Dun he had been converted to total abstinence from both sex and drink. Always a moderate man (Bruce told us) he had decided to enter into his life as a commissioned officer as spare and chaste in habit as a mediaeval knight, whose dedication to duty and contempt of carnality all officers of the King should wish to emulate.

When we pointed out that most knights, however dedicated, had seen no need to go to quite such extremes of asceticism, he replied that he himself was taking the Knights Templar and the Knights Hospitaller as his examples, and that these had been renowned for their abstemious regime and regimen. The Knights Templar, we said, were also renowned for coming to a very sticky end. No doubt the penalty, he rejoined, of their later falling-off from grace.

And so with his plan, such as it was, already in tatters, Jerry led Bruce away to 'meet a special friend of mine', begging the question of why the rest of us were to stay behind with some feeble evasion about lack of space in the Tonga which he had hired for the evening.

'The whole scheme was ridiculous anyway,' said Morgan Grenfell. 'What on earth did he hope was going to happen? That Bruce should be so smitten with this girl that he would instantly abandon himself to lust and then take responsibility for the pregnancy?'

'Something of the kind,' said James. 'He was just setting up a situation and hoping the Devil would lend a helping hand.'

'But the old Bruce would never have fallen for that trick,' I said, 'a moderate man in every sense, as he himself has just been telling us. And as for the new teetotal Bruce, the *sans peur* and *sans reproche* Bruce… What in heaven's name does he think he's letting himself in for anyhow? Where does he think he's going?'

'He's fond of Jerry,' said Giles, 'though God knows why. He wants to see what he's getting up to and then weigh in with some advice. Not before time.'

'It'll take more than advice to sort this Rosalie thing out – whether she's in the club or whether she's not.'

Jerry re-entered Ley Wong's Restaurant.

'I thought you'd still be here,' he said.

'You've only been gone half an hour. What have you done with Bruce?'

'I left him with Rosalie – both of them on their knees, side by side, fervently praying, indeed howling, for God's mercy on the fallen girl. You remember what he said about wanting to be a Knight Templar or something similar?'

'Vividly,' said James.

'Well, the moment he saw Rosalie he started his act. He was her holy knight, he told her, who had come to save her from the Devil and everlasting torment. Could she not see that her whoredoms would soon deliver her to Hell? Let her kneel with him and repent. And she was so impressed, or terrified, or astonished, or spiritually uplifted, that she did just that.'

'Where was all this going on?' said Morgan Grenfell.

'In the lounge bar of the Hotel Maharani.'

'The what?'

'The Hotel Maharani. A rather dubious establishment that admits Eurasians and which for some reason the authorities have not put out of bounds.'

'They went down on their knees in the lounge bar?'

'So did a lot of others who were there. It seems that Bruce, whom we always thought the most ordinary man in the world, has got some gift. Like that absurd Semphill Macpherson woman.'

'Like Christ Himself,' murmured James. 'Why didn't he try it on us? Or on you, Jerry, in the Tonga?'

'Just a guess,' said Morgan Grenfell. 'It could be that he is only inspired to preach his mission by and to women. It's a sort of sexual sublimation. When he sees an attractive woman, he doesn't want to have her in the usual way, he wants to strive for and win her soul.'

'Come to think of it,' said Jerry, 'it was only the women there that responded.'

'There you are, you see. It's a sexual deviation on both sides. Rather like Gladstone and the prostitutes. He got his thrills out of discussing their trade and trying to reform them. It seems that although some of them just charged him so much an hour for answering his questions and pretending to listen to his sermons, others really got a big bang out of making their confession.'

'Doesn't this sort of thing sometimes end in mystic copulation?' asked Barry the Boxer. 'You know, like those monks and nuns in the *Thebaid*, who tempted each other and then succumbed, but were raised to holiness again by the fervour of their repentence?'

'I didn't stay to see,' said Jerry. 'I should say that the probability is that they'll all be themselves tomorrow, after Bruce has gone his way. But the useful thing is that when they reached the peak of hysteria they all started rending their garments – quite an amusing sight – and confessing their sins. Rosalie confessed, in front of many witnesses quite apart from me and Bruce, that she had lied about being pregnant. She asked my forgiveness, which she can have with all my heart. And that, you see, is now that.'

'Funny,' said James. 'It was God Who came to save you when you were counting on the Devil.'

And if Rosalie hadn't been bad enough, Jerry then became infatuated with a polo pony. Or rather, with the idea of a polo pony. Or rather, with the idea of owning and riding a polo pony. Which first had to be bought.

He borrowed the money, 1,500 rupees, from Ley Wong, who acted as private banker to many cadets on a principle of no-interest-but-you-and-your-friends-give-your-parties-at-my-bloody-damn-fine-restaurant. And he bought the pony. And he even played polo (rather well), until it broke its neck in a gymkhana in which it was being ridden, on loan, by our company commander's wife, who refused, being a bitch, to pay up. 'Badly schooled, that pony of yours, young man; wrong footed itself; no fault of mine.' Well, possibly not. No particular worry either, not yet. Jerry was already sick of polo, and as for Ley Wong's Rs 1,500 – well, Ley Wong could wait.

But not forever.

The custom was to pay Ley Wong what one owed by way of restaurant bills and personal loans from the handsome 'pre-commissioning' pay-out which one received about a fortnight before one was actually commissioned. One could then, the official theory was, buy necessary uniforms in preparation and set up funds and arrangements for one's furlough, of which three weeks were due to each newly created second lieutenant. Well and good. But when one had Rs 1,500 to pay for a dead polo pony, the thing was not so easily done. Jerry, of all people, had need of well-cut uniforms (to be had, at a price, in the bazaar of the military cantonment) and had planned a lavish leave. It was going to be a tight fit. Ley Wong must go on waiting. But until when? Until Jerry returned to Bangalore, in transit and awaiting posting, after his leave. Time to worry about this dreary debt then, thought Jerry. No, said Ley Wong: 'Ley

Wong must be paid before cadet Jelly Stanrey receive pletty pip on thoulder.'

'Come, come, man: don't take that disobliging tone with me.'

'Ley Wong must be paid thix days before cadet Jelly Stanrey have paththing-out palade; else Ley Wong must talk with Bligadier Commandant.'

And that was that. Ley Wong's terms were generous but they were absolute: final settlement (the date for which was always made clearly known to all cadets who dealt with him) was not to be fudged or postponed. Since Jerry, in hope of just such a fudge or postponement, had already paid substantial cash deposits from his pre-commissioning money towards his clobber and his hols, there was currently nothing for Ley Wong at all. Yet 'talk with Bligadier Commandant' must be avoided at all costs, as it now appeared (on the authority of a friendly staff-serjeant instructor) that debt, that old abominable scourge of the Raj, was reckoned by the authorities to disqualify a cadet from being commissioned quite as surely as lunacy or death.

'Five things only cause a cadet to fail here,' the staff-serjeant said. 'Demise, irremediable pottiness, pox the third time round and debt.'

'That's only four,' Morgan Grenfell said.

'The other thing is…hard to define. It can be trivial, on the face of it, or evidently damnable. There was an instance, when I first came here, but I was too new to the place to appreciate what was going on. I *do* remember that the cadet concerned was instantly disgraced and sent, as a private soldier, to the nearest battalion of infantry.'

'Yet you can't remember what he'd done, Staff?'

'No.'

'Trivial…or damnable?'

'Depends how you look at it.'

'Surely, in this unique case…however strange you were to the OTS…you must remember what the chap had done.'

'It was an infringement...of security. In general, a pretty obvious crime, you may think. Yet this case might be seen as so petty, until you think about it carefully, that you wouldn't guess in a millennium what that wretched cadet had done, that whatever it was...could conceivably have brought about his dismissal.'

'Come on, Staff. Tell us. We'd be grateful,' said Giles, 'for the warning.'

'That's just why I'm not allowed to tell you. They don't want you to be warned, you see. They consider it is something which a cadet should think of for himself, something a proper potential officer should not need warning about. It is all to do with having unceasing care for the details of discipline, particularly those aspects of discipline that affect security. You have to remember that India always was, and definitely still is, a hostile country in many, perhaps most ways. So have a care for detail, young gentlemen, right up to the time you march past the Commandant on the very last lap.'

There was a long and gloomy silence.

'Why can't you be more concrete?' said Giles.

'I've told you. But we have got one immediate and concrete matter to hand, to which we must now revert. Cadet Stanley's debt to Ley Wong. Somehow or other you must prevent Ley Wong from taking a complaint to the Commandant. If he reports Mr Stanley for not paying up, then it's all UP for Mr Stanley. Abuse of trust...not to be confused with what I've just been talking about, gentlemen. *That* is all...slightly chancy, like an ambush where you least expect it, though expect it you should. This business of Mr Stanley's, on the other hand, is perfectly straightforward: gentlemen must keep their word over money.'

'I have a plan,' Jerry said.

'Oh good,' said James.

'May we know what?' pouted Giles.

'At Bangalore Races this weekend there is a scurry for polo ponies. During my recent polo days, I got to know quite a lot of the local ponies – and their riders. Now, there's a pony called Lars Porsena, ridden by Captain Piers Longshaft of the Mysore Lancers…'

'Gambling,' jeered Giles. 'It will never work.'

'It has been known to,' said Morgan Grenfell.

'*Informed* gambling,' said Barry the Boxer. 'Inside knowledge makes a lot of difference.'

'I need a small loan,' said Jerry. '150 rupees.'

'Let me oblige,' said Morgan Grenfell. 'It runs in the family.'

'What is the exact plan?' asked James.

'Yes,' I repeated. 'What is the *exact* plan?'

'Call it a plan?' quacked Giles. 'He'll just put the money on and hope for the best. I imagine this thing is an outsider,' he said to Jerry, 'or you couldn't win enough to pay Ley Wong.'

'Oh yes,' said Jerry. 'I've already agreed the price with Mr K Veeraswami, turf accountant, of the bazaar. One hundred to six for cash.' He waved Morgan Grenfell's loan in the air. 'So thank you very much for this,' he said. 'How kind. I'll take it along to Veeraswami this evening.'

'I shall expect a commission of ten per cent in case of success,' said Morgan Grenfell. 'That also runs in the family.'

'But your plan can't be as simple as that,' said James. 'Just a straight gamble at long odds?'

'It isn't,' said Jerry. 'The whole point of my plan is that this pony will lose.'

'Yet you'll still put your money on?'

'My money,' said Morgan Grenfell.

'Oh yes,' said Jerry. '150 rupees at 100 to six, call it sixteen to one, makes a nice little win of 2,400…so I shall have a good bit over after I've paid Ley Wong –'

' – and returned my loan with commission – '

' – to deal with all other possible embarrassments.'

'But you said,' nagged Giles, 'that this pony will lose. So how can you win 2,400 rupees on it?'

'It's got to lose before it can win. It can never beat the favourite...which is the fastest job between here and the Malabar Coast, except by coming second and objecting on grounds of having been fouled.'

'Rather difficult to arrange?'

'But not impossible. The thing is, you see, that Piers Longshaft, who owns and rides Lars Porsena, is, as I told you, in the Mysore Lancers. Now, the Mysore Lancers aren't a regular Indian regiment but troops raised by the Maharajah of Mysore. Most of the officers are natives, and both they and the few white officers, like Piers, hold the Maharajah's Commission; not the King Emperor's Commission, nor the Viceroy's, but the Maharajah's.'

'And so?' said Morgan Grenfell.

'They are appointed and dismissed at the Maharajah's pleasure, not subject to British or Indian Military Law, or King's Regulations, or to the Army Council.'

'And so?' said James.

'Wait and see,' said Jerry Stanley.

The favourite for the polo scurry, Wee Willie Winkie, was ridden by its owner, Lieutenant-Colonel Mordaunt Jackson, Commanding Officer of the Third (TA) Battalion of the Pembrokeshire Regiment, which was at that time stationed at Napier Camp, near Bangalore, and employed in support of the Civil Power. A cramped, shrivelled man, Mordaunt Jackson seemed to claw his way on to his pony in the paddock rather than mount it and then chivvy it into a series of crablike, sideways movements to get it on to the sand path which led to the course. Piers Longshaft, on the other hand, mounted with aplomb and rode bravely out like a banneret at the head of his squadron.

'Why is Wee Willie Winkie the favourite?' said Barry the Boxer, 'and Lars Porsena one of the outsiders?'

'Because Lars Porsena is all show,' said Jerry, 'and Wee Willie Winkie is as fast as the Four Horses of the Apocalypse.'

'They're yards apart in the line-up.'

'No draw for a polo scurry.'

'Then why doesn't Lars Porsena get closer to Wee Willie Winkie if it's going to stage a foul?'

'Wait and see.'

Wee Willie Winkie won by a street. Lars Porsena was second, as Jerry's plan required, but at no stage during the race did it come anywhere near Wee Willie Winkie, let alone get in any way impeded or fouled by it.

Colonel Mordaunt Jackson rode into the winner's stall. Captain Longshaft rode up behind him, dismounted, removed one glove, flapped it across the cheek of the Colonel as he walked out of the stall and said, 'My second will wait on yours, Colonel, if you will kindly name him, and they can agree a suitable place. As I am the challenger, you will have choice of weapon.'

'What's this tomfoolery all about?' said Colonel Mordaunt Jackson.

'Nothing more serious, Colonel, I do assure you. I am challenging you to a duel on the ground that you deliberately fouled my pony during the race.'

'Then object to the stewards. I was nowhere near your damn pony.'

'So now you give me the lie. Another cause for a challenge.'

'Officers of His Majesty the King are forbidden to engage in duels of any kind.'

'Officers of His Highness the Maharajah of Mysore are not forbidden. We can fight on neutral territory, where you are not subject to arrest. HH will gladly lend us a corner of his gardens. Or we can fight here on the course, all of which belongs to him.'

'What are you trying to start?' said Jackson. 'You know the form as well as any man in the Indian Peninsula. If you think you've been cheated in this race, you object to the stewards. You don't start waving sabres around.'

Piers Longshaft leaned forward and spoke in Mordaunt Jackson's ear. Jackson stiffened, then nodded. They conferred very briefly, then went off with their saddles and gear to the weighing room. A few minutes later Captain Piers Longshaft's Lars Porsena was announced and posted as the winner. Wee Willie Winkie, it appeared, had weighed in at five pounds under.

'Well, well, well,' said James, 'and what was all that about?'

'Plan B,' said Jerry. 'Plan A, as you know, was that Longshaft should get himself fouled or bumped and claim the race on an objection. That didn't work. Piers couldn't get himself close enough to Jackson in the scrimmage. So then Plan B came into operation. Piers Longshaft issues a public challenge to Mordaunt Jackson to fight a duel with weapons of the latter's choosing. Longshaft can do this with impunity as there is nothing against it in the Maharajah's regulations for the conduct of his officers and the racecourse is the Maharajah's property – his ground. But of course, no matter whose ground it is, Jackson, as a King's officer, cannot accept the challenge. Longshaft knows this very well. He also knows, because I have told him, that Rosalie's mother was employed in the Jackson house, into which she introduced the eleven-year-old Rosalie. Enough said.'

'Blackmail,' said Giles with disgust.

'A gentlemen's agreement: you, Jackson, get rid of some of your weights, say this occurred by accident during racing and honourably cede the race; I, Longshaft, shall say nothing about dear little Rosalie…who is now, incidentally, in an Anglican Convent in Kodykanal, repenting her former sins but still with a very sharp tongue in her head if someone should make trouble and Rosalie be called as a witness.'

'And all that stuff about a duel?' said Morgan Grenfell. 'Why bother with that?'

'A red herring. A false scent to obscure the true one. For public consumption, the story is that Piers knew, or thought he knew, that he had been cheated by Jackson's riding under weight and became so angry when Jackson won that he challenged him. Jackson admits that he has lost some weights but assures Longshaft that this was due to a nasty jolt in riding. The rumour that he *intended* to ride under weight has been put about by a disaffected syce, who has now (rather conveniently) disappeared. Anyway, Jackson gives his word as an officer and a gentleman that the weights were shifted by accident, whereupon the whole thing is amicably settled in the weighing room and Piers gets the race. All plain sailing; a bit of understandably hot temper, but no harm done; no further explanation needed and absolutely no talk of eleven-year-old Rosalie (which nobody concerned really wants) or of anything as horrendous as blackmail. Thus an amusing tale is put about in the clubs and messes instead of the unsavoury truth.'

'Rough on Jackson?' said James. 'Losing his prize.'

'Not really. The prize for that scurry was piffling. And once he is in friendly agreement with Piers Longshaft, Longshaft is happy to give him a few tips (also originating from me) about some unreformed young, very young, friends of Rosalie's who will be happy to meet the distinguished Colonel Mordaunt Jackson. A much nicer prize than a cheque for a hundred chips and a cheap trophy. And I collect my 2,400 from Veeraswami. Something for everybody.'

'Surely not much for Longshaft,' I said. 'As you observed, the race itself is almost worthless.'

'He had a nice big bet on himself. The Maharajah, loyal to one of his officers, had a much bigger bet. The Maharajah will be very pleased with Captain Piers Longshaft. Cheerio for now, chums. I'm off to the bazaar to lift my loot from that old crocodile, Veeraswami.'

'You settle with Ley Wong before you go anywhere to celebrate,' said James.

'I shall go straight to him from Veeraswami's snakepit. Where else should I celebrate but in Ley Wong's restaurant?'

'I think I'll come along,' said Morgan Grenfell, 'to secure my investment. Plus ten per cent of the profit, if I remember aright. But I thought I might waive some of that if we just happened to meet one of Rosalie's little sisters and you were kindly to introduce me...'

'No more of that,' said Jerry. 'We're now into the last furlong and I'm going to take no more risks before we get our commissions.'

'The Devil a saint would be,' scoffed Giles.

'Will *nothing* please you, Giles?' said James. 'Bravo, Jerry. Straight running now till you're past the post.'

On the night before our passing-out parade everyone stayed sober, including Jerry Stanley. We all dined early in the officer cadets' mess, including Jerry Stanley. Virtue was not rewarded. At three in the morning half of us were woken by violent enteritis, in no case more violent than that of Jerry Stanley.

The next morning about a third of those due to pass out that day were excused the actual parade, being afflicted by continuous flux. Among those excused was, of course, Jerry Stanley.

'Don't forget,' said James, who was unaffected by the pest, 'to hand your rifles in.'

As junior under officer of our platoon, he was quite properly reminding us of the last procedure we must complete as cadets. Our rifles, which were kept in a guarded arms kote for reasons of security, must be taken out, cleaned and formally presented to the kote orderly (a senior Indian NCO) who would certify the weapons as being in the correct condition and then strike them off our personal charge. Normally this would be done immediately after the passing-out parade; but those who were not to appear on the POP because of illness were commanded, by standing orders of the OTS, to attend the arms kote for the handing in procedure during the parade itself, thus reducing the stampede at its conclusion.

A simple task, cleaning one's weapon and handing it over a counter to be checked and signed for by a responsible Indian orderly; not so simple, however, if one had diarrhoea like Vindaloo curry.

True to his resolution to run straight until the end, Jerry Stanley cleaned his rifle with care and accuracy, down to the last finicking notch of the foresight. Then, 'Christ,' he said to me as we stood in the queue to hand our arms over, 'I've got to trot. Hold my rifle for me just a mo.'

Jerry trotted. I held his rifle for him, along with my own. Giles, who had been ahead of us in the queue and had now completed the formalities, passed me on his way out.

'Two rifles?' he said. 'What's the trouble?'

Here I should explain that the rifles at Bangalore were old and faulty, and that very often cadets had to be issued with a second while the first was kept permanently in the kote awaiting repair by the armourer, who sometimes took weeks before he got round to it. When this occurred, one would have two rifles on one's charge and it was one's duty, if this was still the case at the time of passing out, to clean and hand back both to the orderly, who would then strike both off one's charge. Clearly, this was what Giles thought was happening here and it was the merest whim that had prompted his question.

'Which one is out of order,' he said now, 'and why? Someone really ought to make a report,' he continued pompously, 'about the poor state of the weaponry at this OTS.'

Bored with this inconsequent silliness, nerves fluttering and bowels simmering, I said, 'For Christ's sake, Giles, buzz off.'

'As cadet platoon Serjeant, I'm only taking a proper interest in the state of the platoon's rifles.'

'There's nothing wrong with either of these,' I said. 'One of them is Jerry Stanley's.'

'And where is Stanley?'

'In the bog just over there.'

'Leaving his rifle unguarded.' Giles took a deep breath. His face began to swell like a balloon.

'Not unguarded,' I said. 'With me.'

'You know the regulations in this country. Except when a man's rifle is locked away in the arms kote, he is responsible for keeping it with him at all times. It is not a responsibility that can be delegated.'

'For Christ's sake, Giles.'

Jerry appeared.

'I'm afraid some got away before I got there,' he said. 'I'll have to go back to the basha [quarters] and change my knickers. I suppose I'd better take my rifle in case you get to the counter before I'm back.'

'Officer Cadet Stanley,' said Giles. 'It is my duty to inform you that I am now placing you under close arrest for failing to keep your personal weapon under proper surveillance.'

'It's like I said the other day, gentlemen,' said the friendly Staff-Serjeant instructor at the passing-out party. 'There's certain breaches of discipline or security that they never forgive out here. Little things, you might think; but things that have so often cost good men's lives. You're on the Frontier, right? You leave your rifle with a mate for two ticks while you go for a crap. You're caught by Fuzzi Khan with your trousers down, you can't defend yourself or give warning, the whole company is butchered by Fuzzi and his pals...'

'But Staff,' said James. 'This business of Jerry Stanley's occurred in peace time, in the secure arms kote of a secure barracks in a secure garrison town – '

' – The point about a rule, sir, is that you obey it all the time. Even when it doesn't matter, in case you start getting careless and forget it when it does.'

'Then you see no hope that they might let Jerry Stanley off and allow him to take up his commission?'

'None at all, sir. And in my view, rightly not.'

'Did Giles do it out of spite?' said James to me as we walked back to our basha from the party. 'Or did he think, like that Staff-Serjeant, that a drill must be a drill forever and in all circumstances?'

'Giles did not approve of Jerry. He did not think that he should be allowed to get away with things. Jerry has got away with rather a lot during this course.'

'The worst problem, now,' said James, 'is that they are *not* sending Jerry away to another unit as a private soldier. He's to stay with us. Come on commissioning leave with us. Still as a cadet.'

'But – '

' – Clement Attlee is keeping his promise and bringing the boys home. We are *all* going home when we've been on leave, as are all the battalions out here to which we might have been posted. So it is administratively convenient, the company commander told me, to send Jerry back with us. He wants us to take care of him.'

'What do we do about Giles? We must keep them apart.'

'Mercifully, Giles is going to spend his furlough with grand cousins, near Madras. So Jerry can come with us to Ooty.'

'Hadn't he made plans of his own?'

'He won't have the money to follow them up. Now he's not to be commissioned, they'll be screwing him to pay the advances and allowances back.'

'Then he can't even afford Ooty.'

'That will be seen to,' said munificent James.

'So all will be well – during our leave?'

'Yes.'

'But then…?'

'Then we shall all have to report to the transit camp at Deolali, to await passage home. A draft of 299 newly commissioned second lieutenants, and the one failure, Officer Cadet (for that is to be his style until further notice) Jerry Constant Stanley.'

Officer Cadet Jerry Constant Stanley was subdued and agreeable while we were on leave. Since we did not wear uniform, he did not stand out as the odd man. He didn't seem to resent his calamity. He never referred to the absent Giles.

'I don't like it,' said Morgan Grenfell, who was helping James to see that there was ample and tactful management in the matter of Jerry's expenses. 'Why should he be so calm when he's been served a dirty turn like that? One would have expected him to be raging and shouting all day long.'

'That would not be dignified. He always had an odd sense of his dignity, whatever he was up to. And it would not be polite to his hosts. Although flamboyant and flashy, he always had considerate manners. It explains much of his success.'

'It did,' said Barry the Boxer.

'I hope he's all right at Deolali,' said Morgan Grenfell. 'You know there's a thing called Deolali Tap? It's a sort of madness people get when they're kept there too long without a passage and without any orders. They begin to feel they don't exist. They think they have to do something – anything – in order to draw attention to themselves before they finally vanish into thin air.'

'So long as we are with Jerry, and treat him just like one of ourselves, he will be all right,' James said. 'He will be with us in Deolali and then on the boat. After that we really cannot be answerable.'

It had all been my fault. If I had only, when Giles asked about the two rifles I was holding, just agreed that they were both in my charge for a perfectly commonplace and respectable reason, then all would have been well. But no. I wasn't well and I wasn't thinking straight that morning. I was sick and tired of Giles. I wanted peace. So I told him what appeared at the time to be a perfectly harmless truth — that I was looking after Jerry's rifle for him while he went to the loo, which was ten yards away, just over the floor of the rifle kote.

What had got into Giles? He'd barely been seen since the day of our commissioning. He had attended the party, been treated with suspicion and reserve (but not incivility) by all present, and had then left to join his smart connections on the coast south of Madras. He had said nothing to his friends before leaving, had indeed said nothing to anybody, save for his oral report while delivering Jerry to the guard house, since Jerry's arrest. He had no need even to give evidence, for Jerry was never formally charged. Neither he nor anyone else could deny what had happened; rather than get up a court martial with all the fuss and pain of it, the Commandant had simply pronounced, as he was fully entitled to (back in 1947) without giving any particular reason, that Officer Cadet Stanley, J. C., was unfit to become an officer and that was that. The authorities did not like cadets being failed at Bangalore after the expense (as we have seen) of getting them there, but one cadet out of 300, for there was no other, was an acceptable ratio. The whole affair was therefore being very coolly passed off.

'Firm but not vindictive,' was James' judgement of the authorities' behaviour (though not of Giles'), 'yet obviously obsessive. You,' he said to me, 'are not to blame. How could you know that Giles would turn Judas or that the army in India is still living in the era of the Mutiny?'

So although it had all been my fault for saying what I did, morally, it appeared, it was not my fault at all. James' word, in such matters, was conclusive. But what was to happen next?

Not culpable though I might be, I must surely, like everyone else, take an interest in the outcome. Neither the absent Giles nor the taciturn Jerry had given any indication of personal feeling and intention, but feeling and intention, on both sides, there must be, and surely no longer to be disguised when Second Lieutenant Giles Benson was confronted by Officer Cadet Jerry Stanley in the officers' mess (which Jerry, under the present dispensation, would be allowed to use) in the transit camp at Deolali, celebrated for Deolali Tap.

But in the event there was no confrontation, or not of the kind we expected. James, Morgan Grenfell, Barry the Boxer, Jerry and I returned from our furlough in the Nilgeri Hills to the OTS at Bangalore. There we were given documents and orders, and after two days took the train for Deolali. Giles, we had heard from the friendly Staff-Serjeant Instructor, who made it his business to know such things, had been taken ill at the home of his influential relatives. These telephoned the Commandant of the OTS to seek an extension of leave for Giles, who was reputedly too ill to telephone for himself.

So what was the matter with Giles? we enquired.

Well, according to the ORQMS, who had overheard the Commandant's end of the telephone call, Giles had dysentery, not just the sporadic and annoying diarrhoea (Bangalore belly) common among all British troops in the garrison, but real, red-hot dysentery that went through a man like a ray gun. Then the situation was as follows, the Commandant had instructed Giles' host: Giles was due to return to the OTS, to collect his documents and then proceed to Deolali, not later than three days hence; if, therefore, he was still unfit to travel by then, Giles must be placed in the military hospital in Madras and he (the Commandant) must be notified that this had been done. In this way the whole matter would be put on an official basis, and responsibility for Giles would have been correctly and satisfactorily shifted. Thus the business stood when we boarded the train for Deolali; and when we arrived there three days later we heard from the head clerk in Postings that Giles had indeed been moved into the military hospital at Madras and was not expected to reach Deolali in time to catch the troopship on which the rest of us were to embark for England, home and beauty from nearby Bombay.

'Well,' said Morgan Grenfell in the ramshackle junior officers' mess, 'that's one embarrassment out of the way.'

Jerry came in.

'Can't come in here, boy,' said the mess Serjeant. Only officers in here. Hop it.'

James tactfully explained what had been decreed about Jerry and his status. The mess Serjeant listened crossly but condescended to serve Jerry.

'I've had a letter,' Jerry said. 'From those relatives of Giles Benson's who had him to spend his leave with them. They say he wanted to write to me but was much too weak. He wanted to write and say he was sorry for sneaking on me. It's been troubling him. He now thinks (according to these people at Madras) that he acted out of spite, impulsive spite. He was jealous about my way of enjoying life and avoiding the consequences. He wanted to give me a lesson. *Et cetera.* So now he's ill and he's sorry, and he wants to be forgiven. I must write, say these friends of his, to Giles at the British military hospital, Madras and say I forgive him everything.'

'Who exactly are these "friends" or "relatives"?'

'Distant cousins, I gather,' said Jerry, 'a husband and wife and their daughter, to whom Giles was apparently going to be engaged. Later, when they were both a little older. They'd known each other before the war, in the nursery, while they were growing up. *Et cetera.* The man wrote the letter, and his wife and daughter added postscripts. The daughter's was particularly affecting. "This guilt about what he has done to you is making Giles far worse," she writes. "Please save him for me. I feel he may die unless you write. He gets weaker every day.

All he talks of when we go to see him is his wickedness to you. He is obsessed. Only you can cure him of his obsession." '

'What are you going to do?' asked James.

'I shall write. Of course I must.'

'Good man.'

'But I shall not write at once,' said Jerry. 'Clearly it is a letter that will have to be composed very carefully.'

But before he could write, the daughter, Giles' fiancée to be, arrived, to intercede with Jerry personally. He was given leave to go and meet her in the Taj-Mahal Hotel in Bombay.

'She helped me to compose the letter,' said Jerry, when he got back to Deolali the next day. 'Marjorie — that's her name — will go straight back to Madras and deliver it to Giles in person. Can't think what he sees in her: stupid, dumpy, snobby little bitch. Fell into my arms. Hot for anything I'd give her — though she wouldn't allow *it*. Says she's keeping herself pure for her husband.'

'For Giles?'

'No. For me. I've got to take care of my future, chums. I'm sailing home with no commission, no prospects inside the army or out. I can do with a really influential father-in-law. He'll be back in England almost as soon as we shall be — he's only here on a three-month tour of duty for his firm. Marjorie says he can get me out of the army early — industrial priority of some kind. You see what sort of post-war world it's going to be, if bloody rubbish of that sort is going to take precedence over the service. Ah, well. The job he'll find me will be desperately boring but exceedingly well paid.'

'What about Marjorie?' Morgan Grenfell said.

'What about her?'

' "Stupid, dumpy, snobby…" '

'She'll be a loyal wife and a good mother. She's randy but she means what she says about purity. I don't object to that…in a wife.'

'What shall you tell Giles?'

'It's all in the letter which Marjorie's taking to him. Oh yes, I forgive him all right. He's fucked up my commission, he's reduced me to the ranks, once we get home, for the rest of my National Service, sentenced me to subordination and misery and discomfort. But I've forgiven him, I've written, because he's brought me and Marjorie together: Marjorie will make up for everything. I haven't spelt it out – I couldn't, of course, with her breathing over my shoulder – but he'll know what I mean.'

'Mightn't this kill him?'

'Oh no. They all said he was dying of weakness made worse by remorse, that he was dying of guilt because of the way he's treated me. Now that things have turned out so well for me after all, he can hardly feel remorse or guilt any more; so he can throw off his weakness and live. Not many people die of dysentery these days. Let him pull himself together: it was what he was always recommending to others.'

Giles died in the military hospital at Madras from amoebic dysentery, probably exacerbated by outrage and loss of face. This would not have occurred, for Jerry would never have met Marjorie and there would have been no shock to render Giles' illness fatal, had not he committed a mean and treacherous act of delation; so justice of a kind was done.

Jerry, the freebooter, married squat Marjorie, was placed in dull but opulent circumstances and fell ill of a cancer. He would have been dead within months, but Marjorie, who loved him, used her money on treatments to keep him alive, until he was pleading for death and her entire portion was spent.

Much of all this, and that the worst of it, would never have happened if only I'd behaved sensibly when Giles Benson commented on my having two rifles in my care and if only I'd gone along with the plausible explanation which he himself suggested, instead of insisting on telling the truth. I can't even claim I did this out of habit, as I more often than not told lies – one is apt to, in the army. Perhaps I wanted to kill a few moments of waiting in a boring queue (desiring not peace, as I once thought, but distraction) or perhaps I wanted to remind Giles that even he did not know everything. In any case, I said what I said without thinking or noticing or caring – so utterly trivial was the whole affair – and thereby set in train a sequence of events that ended in protracted agony for Jerry Stanley (instead of the quick and early death that would normally have been his lot) and an unhallowed decease for Giles Benson.

PART TWO

The Man of Probity

I first met the man of probity in Rome, at the top end of the Via Vittorio Veneto. He was small in stature, uneasily contained in girth and Hebraic in countenance. He had black eyes, rather protuberant, which were suspicious, disapproving and unhappy. All in all, he was an unattractive man, and it was difficult for me to understand why two of the most fastidious and intelligent men of my year at King's should be in his company.

I stopped to talk to them. I had the impression that they would much sooner that I hadn't; but civility, to say nothing of friendship, required them to notice me – and to introduce me to Mr Joseph Goldstein.

'Ah,' I said fatuously. 'This is your man with the yacht.'

For now I remembered that for some time there had been talk of how Ian Beauclerc and Donald McComb had found a rich patron to take them on a tour this spring (1952), a man who had been vaguely and rather disparagingly referred to by them as 'our man with the yacht'. And now here they all were. There should, I remembered, be two adopted and motherless daughters of widower Goldstein somewhere around. These, if I had it right, were sixteen and twenty, and it was to amuse them that Ian and Donald had been invited. Speculation as to where they were now (still in bed at 11.45 am?) was interrupted by Mr Goldstein, who said bleakly, 'I have no yacht.'

'Sorry, sir,' I said. 'Just a silly joke.'

The affronted Goldstein jutted his sharp little chin, raised his hooter and strutted away down the golden pavement. Ian and Donald, shifty and sycophantic, prepared to follow.

'Meet us at Doney's at six p.m.,' said Ian. 'That's when we have our hour off.'

'Twenty thousand lire a day pocket money,' said Ian that evening, as we waited at a table inside Doney's for our drinks. ('It's much too common to sit outside with all those jostling whores,' Donald had said.) 'Lunch every day with Jo, which is what he likes to be called, and the two girls – who mercifully spend the whole morning at the hairdresser. Culture after lunch with the girls – only most culture is shut all the afternoon and by the time it's open again the girls are having their *cinq à sept*. That's why we're here now.'

'Any money to spare?' I said.

'No. But we'll buy all the drinks.'

'What about dinner?'

'Heavily on duty again, I'm afraid. Chloë and Sammy and Jo like a smart dinner (as opposed to a good one) and at least one nightclub.'

'Sammy?'

'The younger one. Jo wanted a boy, but the adoption shop hadn't got one – even for ready money.'

'No chums invited?'

'Not,' said Donald, 'when they've made cretinous remarks about yachts.'

'Nothing in this for me then?' I said. 'Nothing at all?'

'Just keep out of our way,' said Ian. 'I think I've got something going here.'

Ian was poor; Donald was not. Ian, as he told me, was Chloë's cavalier; Donald was a kind of older brother to Sammy.

'How does this Jo get his money?' I asked.

'He's a lawyer,' said Donald. 'He looks after trusts. A lot of his business is in Europe, so he has no problems over currency.' In 1952 this was a very special recommendation. 'In return for the first decent trip abroad since Mum took me to Provence in 1938, when I was fourteen, I am content to play tutor to Sammy and pretend she's a boy, which is what Jo likes. And that is all, but it's not too bad at that. So don't you come buggering it up. Jo's got your number: he hates scroungers.'

'Scrounger yourself.'

'*Touché*,' sighed Donald.

'But Ian, I gather, is in it for more than the ride.'

'Yes,' said Ian. 'Chloë wants me. It remains to be seen what price Jo will pay.'

Back in England that summer, it was clear that Ian was the one who must pay the price. Nothing would come to him with the hand of Chloë except a matrimonial chamber and a tiny dressing room in Joseph Goldstein's house – not even a separate flat, for the newly weds must live with Goldstein, so to speak, *en suite*. Other conditions were even more distasteful: although Chloë had a liberal settlement from her adoptive father, her bridegroom would have nothing but a sparse salary in respect of working as an apprentice lawyer in the firm of Goldstein and Brucke, Solicitors, while studying to become a solicitor himself. On all this Goldstein insisted. Ian was also to sever relations with all old Cambridge friends like myself ('scroungers and parasites') though he was allowed to retain the friendship of Donald of whom, because of Donald's money, Goldstein approved. Travel would cease for Ian except during his three weeks' annual holiday; cultural or literary pursuits were discouraged, as he would be expected to spend such free time as he had in escorting Chloë to the fashionable exhibitions and popular light entertainments on which she had been reared; and while a fair standard of eating and drinking was permitted when Ian was in Chloë's company, any retrogression to 'bachelor excesses or extravagance' was of course outlawed. 'It remains to be seen,' Ian had said on that evening in Doney's, 'what price Jo will pay.' The answer was merely a home of sorts and a job as a legal drudge. Thin gruel and bitter bread. Why had Ian accepted? we all asked ourselves.

'Three reasons,' said Donald, as he walked with me by the Serpentine a week before the wedding. 'First, Ian had to do *something*; he couldn't go on for ever lolling round London getting drunk on credit. Second, he is impressed by Goldstein, by the power and success of the man, even more, perhaps, by his doctrine of hard work and honesty as the sole begetters of happiness and wealth. Ian has been got to see himself, for the time at least, as the industrious apprentice who will ride, one day, in the Lord Mayor's coach.'

Donald paused to observe the water fowl with a mixture of compassion and disdain.

'And the third reason?' I prompted.

'Chloë herself. He doesn't love her, of course, but he is amused by her, by her dainty little-girl airs and whimsies, contrasted with her absolute relentlessness in getting her own way. He also suspects that there is some incestuous attraction between Chloë and Jo – or rather, a sexual hankering, on both sides, that would be incestuous if Chloë weren't adopted. This intrigues him. He looks forward to watching them together and also to watching the way that Sammy makes a bid for Jo's affection by playing up to him as a kind of devoted study fag.'

'I dare say these spectacles are curious in their way; but is a ringside seat for them worth the total sacrifice of his freedom?'

'Sacrifice of his freedom? At the moment Ian sees this marriage as cosy security from want or debt. No more duns hammering at the door. No more sweating lest the next post bring news that yet another cheque has been returned by the bank. A quiet, ordered, useful life, with agreeable aspects of domesticity and the prospect of a brilliant career, or at least of an honourable occupation. And there is one more handsome and immediate benefit,' Donald said. 'Before the time of labour and temperance begins, there is to be an interlude of high pleasure. To dull any sense of objection that might still survive in Ian, Jo has arranged a glittering wedding tour for him and Chloë, a whole six weeks of cruising in luxury over the most delectable regions of southern Europe and the Near East. Ian, as you know, was always a man to be tempted by a seductive short-term bribe and it seems that the promise of such a honeymoon has almost obliterated his awareness of the dreary waste that lies at the other end of it.'

And so, in the early autumn, in a church among the Kentish orchards, Ian and Chloë were wed. Jo had set up marquees in his garden and provided princely refreshments in them. He had agreed to entertain, for the first and last time, 'the scroungers and parasites' who had been Ian's companions and were now permitted to be present to witness his transformation from wayward Cherubino to true and dedicated knight.

'Service and duty,' Jo Goldstein said to those around him at the wedding, 'these are the worthwhile things in life, and though they are their own reward, they may bring others – such as this champagne, or the magnificent journey which is my present to Ian and Chloë.'

'In that case,' said Sammy, a little rash with the wine, 'Ian is receiving the reward before producing the service or the duty.'

'He is committed,' Jo Goldstein said.

I slipped away from the outskirts of the group to have a pee in the house. When I came out, the going-away car was waiting by the front door and Goldstein was treading angrily round it, armed with a pair of kitchen scissors and snipping the cords from which dangled old boots and other hymeneal paraphernalia.

'Hateful,' he said to me. 'Hateful.'

'Somebody's idea of a joke,' I said, for once firmly on his side...until he spoke again:

'All the same, these Cambridge friends of Ian's. Nothing sacred to them. No idea of what is sublime or noble.' Snip, snip, snip. 'Frivolous, slothful, sneering. No sense of duty, of effort, of honour.'

Ah well, I thought: let's see how long Ian lasts the course – after the glamorous honeymoon.

Six weeks later, as soon as Ian and Chloë were back from their 'magnificent journey', Ian was conscripted into the daily round of dreariness in Joseph Goldstein's chambers. On the first day of Ian's drudgery Chloë summoned Donald to luncheon.

'Something quite ghastly happened in Palermo,' Chloë said.

'Oh?'

'Everything had gone quite well till then. Comfortable journeys, planned by Daddy, pleasant hotels, arranged by Daddy, carefully chosen meals, paid for out of the money provided by Daddy – it all went well enough. In Florence, we hired a car and drove to Scylla and crossed to Sicily. We had to spend a night in a hotel on the north coast en route to Palermo. A bad hotel and a horrid dinner, but Ian was still happy, unnaturally happy indeed, feverish and gleeful. "We must have contrasts," he said skittishly, "like the young man in that story of Oscar Wilde's who got bored with good wine and had to have bad for a change." The next morning we went on to Palermo. And that evening, in our suite in the Grand Hotel Proserpina, it happened.'

'What happened?' Donald said.

'Something so horrible that I don't think I can bear to tell you about it.'

'You'll have to do better than that,' said Donald in the avuncular manner in which he had been accustomed to address Chloî in the three or four years he had known her. 'You can't tell me that something horrible happened and then not say what it was. That's teasing. And unfair to Ian. It sets up dreadful suspicions but makes it impossible for one to judge. Did he *do* something or did he *say* something?'

'Both. He pretended that he was Daddy and I was Sammy – '

'Was he drunk?'

'No. He'd had a siesta after lunch and ordered some tea and mineral water. He was having his in bed and I was having mine on the balcony…looking over the sea. Suddenly he called out, "It's getting stiff, Sammikins. Come and play with Daddy's thing." '

'Only a joke,' said Donald. (Though as he told me later, when passing on Chloë's story, it was the sort of joke which made him laugh only on one side of his face.) 'A man's joke,' Donald said. 'Now you're married, you'll have to get used to men's jokes.'

'The horrible thing was – it made me feel excited.'

'Then you ought to be grateful.'

'No. It was wicked. Even though Jo's not our real father, it was wicked. And apart from anything else, Ian was laughing at Jo.'

Ian went on laughing at Jo. Very soon he started laughing at Chloë too. He laughed at law and he laughed at Jo Goldstein's practice. He laughed at Jo's elderly clients, who relied on Jo to keep their trusts in order, and he laughed at Jo's righteous accounts of how meticulously he controlled their affairs and of how dependent they were on Jo for livelihood and even love.

'I cherish them,' said Jo. 'They are like my children.'

Ian laughed.

'I wonder,' said Donald to me in November, 'what can have happened to Ian. He used to be so respectful of Jo, so grateful to him. Now he just jeers at him behind his back and giggles to his face.'

'I haven't seen Ian much since the marriage,' I said. 'Chloë's seen to that. But I gather he now finds Jo an unctuous little windbag. He should have spotted it earlier, before he married that pampered girl of his.'

Donald was miffed. Jo had been his friend, the girls had been his 'nieces' for some years before he had introduced Ian…who now seemed to be mocking them to pieces.

'He insulted Chloë during the honeymoon,' Donald said. 'That business in Palermo I told you about. All the trouble started then. Everything was all right until they reached Palermo. Then, that very afternoon –'

'–Something must have happened on the way to Palermo,' I said.

'Chloë says they had to stay at a nasty hotel on the coast road from Messina. Ian didn't mind — in fact he positively and perversely enjoyed it, Chloë says. Then they went on to Palermo the next day and that very afternoon Ian insulted her. He implied that both Chloë and her sister had an incestuous thing with Jo. That they used…to play with him.'

'It would be in a very ancient tradition,' I said. 'Have you ever seen Cezanne's picture of Lot and his daughters? One of them — a ginger job — is riding the old man in great style and kissing him avidly on the mouth. The second girl is sitting there starting to masturbate, hardly able to wait for her own turn… Moral: incest can be fun. Anyway, what's she getting so het up about? She isn't Jo's real daughter; neither is Sammy.'

'Even so, she thinks Ian's insinuations are wicked. I told you what she said about that.'

'It's probably just a test that Ian has devised. The best thing she can do is have a good laugh and sit on Ian's knee.'

'I find you greatly lacking in moral sense,' said Donald.

'I never claimed to have any. The trouble with the rich is that they have too much time to brood about themselves. Chloë had better get herself together. There'll probably be a lot more tests coming her way before long. She'd better not think that she's going to have it all her own way. Nor Jo either.'

'Considering how much Jo is paying for their keep,' said Donald, taking the side of the rich among whom he was numbered, 'I think Ian might show himself more considerate, more grateful. He's not doing me any good either. It was me that introduced him there, as you know — but do you know why? It was for Ian's good: I was hoping that Jo and the girls would take him in hand and rescue him from the hole he was in. And so they did — but now look.'

'You should have read the Classics at Cambridge,' I told him, 'instead of all that rubbish in German and Russian. Then you might have had the sense to mind your own business. There's nothing like an overdose of Dostoevsky to encourage silly habits like pity and interference.'

For the first time since he got back from his wedding tour, Ian rang me up. It seemed that the next evening Chloë and Jo had been asked to the opera by a client of Jo's.

'Because of some slip-up there's no ticket for me, thank God,' said Ian. 'My first evening off since the altar. I've arranged with Hugo and Margaret that we shall go to the Savoy for dinner. They've got some fresh *foie gras* [at that time, before every tenth-rate restaurant in France produced some grey-green muck under that designation, a rare and sumptuous delicacy]. Then we'll go to a *boîte*, like the old days, when we ran up from Cambridge for the night. I've been helping myself to Chloë's handbag, so I'm going to stand us all.'

Margaret was an old flame of Ian's. Hugo was a Cambridge friend who had married her. A more subversive get-together, from the point of view of the Goldstein camp, could not have been conceived. The party started superbly: fresh *foie gras*, eggs in a lobster sauce under a canopy of cheese soufflé, and woodcock.

'Right,' said Ian. 'Off to the Astor. I've left Chloë a note to say I'll be late.'

'Is this wise?' said Hugo.

'It is perfectly civil. What more can she expect?'

While Hugo and Margaret were dancing to Edmundo Ross' music in the Astor, I said to Ian, 'What happened on the road to Palermo?'

'Nothing much.'

'Come, come. You were happy on your honeymoon, so Chloë told Donald. You were happier than ever in a cheap hotel on the north coast of Sicily, just after you'd crossed. The next day you went on to Palermo to the Proserpina – and there you got up a kind of incest fantasy about Sammy and Jo that pretty well derailed Chloë. So what happened between Scylla and Palermo to set that off?'

I'm a fine one to have lectured Donald about how he should mind his own business, I thought. But at least I'm acting out of honest human curiosity and not in any creepy pretence about doing good.

'Nothing much happened, as I said. What did happen was something to do with that cheap hotel…which was quite charming in a crumbly way but upset my ridiculous, stuck-up wife. Made her go all whiney. This finally opened my eyes – though God knows they should never have closed. I just woke up in the morning to the truth. All right, I told myself: you were beginning to long for relief or at least respite from being a rotter; but what on earth made you sell out to that sanctimonious Goldstein, with his prate about work and duty, and his deadly dull if passably good-looking daughter? When I get back from this wedding trip, I thought, it's going to be grind, grind, grind in one beastly office or another for the rest of my life. And in the evenings there will only be a boring, fudgy room to go to in Goldstein's dreary shit-coloured house. The highlight of my life will be the occasional middle-brow play. So I'd sold out for nothing, worse than nothing. I'd confounded freedom from debt and financial worry with the true freedom – which is to come and go at one's pleasure and to speak as one finds. In short, the sooner I was rid of Jo and Chloë, the better. How to get out? Mock them, that was the only way. The likes of Jo and Chloë can't stand mockery – it makes nonsense of everything they hold to, you see, particularly money. From then on, I told myself, in that dawn on the Sicilian coast, from then on I'd mock the Goldsteins. Then I'd get free.'

'You thought this – after three weeks of marriage?'

'A marriage of desperation, dear boy.'

'Why the incest bit, about Jo and Sammy?'

'To poke naughty fun at Sammikins, as Jo sometimes calls her. Mind you, she was the best of the bunch and wouldn't give a damn, even if she heard about it; but it would infuriate Chloë, prissy, prudish and prurient madam. They both fancy Jo, you see. Why shouldn't they? Lots of women fancy those stubby, greasy Levantine numbers and as for the morals of it, well, they're only adopted. In Rome, on our little gyro last spring, I caught Sammy nestling under his eiderdown; they were having brekker off the same tray and she was reading to him from the newspaper. In Athens I happened to come in while Chloë was giving him a pretty intimate massage. All perfectly legal, if they're only adopted, but good material for mockery… particularly with a po-faced pair like Jo and Chloë.'

'Not very kind.'

'I don't feel kind, dear boy. They snapped me up when I was down for the count. Not a penny in the bank and only that footling job with Tommy Layton's fifth eleven wine firm. So they scraped me out of the mud when I was unconscious, cleaned me up and took me over, and when I came to they'd got me. Caught in their horrible trap. I'm not going to be too fussy about how I fiddle or fight my way out of it. In fact,' Ian said, as Hugo and Margaret reeled off the floor to the strains of Edmundo's signature tune (Mantovani would come on next), 'I'm planning a very big coup for tonight. Drink up,' he said, brandishing the gin bottle (which in those days had a measure gummed down one side of it). 'They'll take this away at two-thirty.'

'Hadn't we better go? I mean, Chloë will be worried.'

'I told you: I left a message to warn her I'd be late. If that's not good enough for her, let her worry till her head drops off.'

'I think,' I said, as Hugo and Margaret slumped down on the banquette, 'that of the two girls I should have chosen Sammy. The best of the bunch, as you say — and from what I saw at your wedding. Snub nose, bitten nails and a few jolly little pimples. Although you tell me she spends half the day in beauty parlours and hairdressers' salons, there is no denying a piquant scruffiness in Sammy, a whiff of adolescence…'

'Have you heard,' said Margaret, 'about Hugo's Mum Rosamond in Venice with Willie?'

'Oh God,' said Hugo.

'Both thought the other had a lot of lire,' Margaret went on, 'Rosamond because Willie travels on some sort of art racket and is as rich as Midas anyway, and Willie because Rosamond gets a special currency allowance for established writers. So they really live it up in Venice, a private boat from the Gritti to Torcello, Harry's for luncheon, the lot. But when the bills came in, they both started trying to borrow from each other; it turned out that they'd both been so mean that despite all their allowances and so on neither of them had a penny beyond what they needed for bare subsistence in a low-grade *pensione*. It was seeing each other that gave them such silly ideas *de luxe*.'

'What did they do?'

'They tried BB, but he wasn't parting with a farthing. Luckily Harold came to Venice and rescued them, then wheeled them off to Florence for a free month at his Palazzo.'

'To them that have,' I said bitterly.

'Cheer up,' said Ian. 'It's none of it really worth having.'

While it had been clear at the Astor that Ian was planning something fairly reckless, I was certainly not prepared for the news which Donald McComb pumped out days later.

'Disaster,' said Donald. 'All your fault, Ian says. You suggested it.'

'Suggested what?'

'Sammy Goldstein.'

'Rubbish. I never suggested anything of the kind.'

'*You* said how attractive she was in a grubby, *gamin* way. *You* set Ian thinking of gym-slips and black stockings with inky thighs still growing out of them.'

'I...I...it was only a *joke*.'

'A rare joke it has turned out to be. Do you know what Ian did when you dropped him at Jo Goldstein's at after three in the morning?'

'Passed out, I should think. That's what I did. On the stairs.'

'No such luck for Ian. When he arrived home he got up the stairs all right. The wrong stairs. Not the stairs which led to his bower of married bliss, but the one that led to Sammy Goldstein's dear little dorm…where she was at least tolerably pleased to see him, though for a while she pretended not to be. "And swearing she would ne'er consent, consented," as Byron has it. And lo and behold, while she is busy crying no, no, no, and lifting the bedclothes to admit him, in comes Chloë just as Ian's knickers plunge to his ankles and leads him straight off to her father's room, his ankles still manacled by his Y-fronts and his manhood more rampant than ever (there can be, you know, a terrific thrill in being caught) to exhibit the beastly priapic spectacle to Daddy.

' "This was what I found in Sammy's bedroom. Raping her."

' "Not raping her," said Ian with satisfaction.

' "O vile. Accusing my little sister of such filth."

'At this stage she begins to notice that there is something very funny, and not ha, ha, about Daddy, whose head is hanging over the side of the bed as if his neck has been snapped. Oh dear, oh dear. Daddy has had a stroke and is dead before Ian's phallus subsides. All *your* fault for putting Sammy into Ian's drunken head.'

What happened next, however, could certainly not be blamed on me.

Jo being dead, his accounts, records, files were opened and examined. For some years, it appeared, this man of probity had been embezzling the funds entrusted to him. He had invested all monies that came his way in the course of his good work in a 'company' which was in fact himself and took care to pay out generous 'dividends' from his accumulated loot, so that no awkward questions should be asked. Since his personal expenditure was high (Belgravian houses and annual boxes for Cheltenham and Ascot did not come cheap even then, to say nothing of extensive European tours for family and friends), he might have been hard put to it to disburse the next round of dividends, due in a month's time.

But by then he would probably have gathered in a fresh load of lucre, as several clients, whose wills he would administer, were heading hard for black Hades. He was, of course, depending on such subventions to continue and to refund him indefinitely, and to this end he had recruited Ian, hoping that his youth and charm would pull in a never-failing series of succulent and trusting geriatrics.

How long the supply of oldies would have lasted, how successful Ian would have been in renewing it, we shall never now know. This, at least, we can record: that Ian (against whom Chloë commenced an immediate action for divorce) was cleared by the police of any knowledge of Jo's fraudulent proceedings, though he had already begun, inadvertently, to assist in finding victims; that Chloë honourably handed over many rich gifts from her 'father' to help the Law Society to compensate Jo's gulls; and that she and her sister then vanished overnight. However, it has been rumoured over the years that Chloë herself married a shady Dutch jeweller, a familiar of Jo's, whom she had met at the beginning (Amsterdam) of the great spring bonanza of 1952, and that Sammy became the secretary of an elderly peer, who liked her to wear an Eton collar and jacket during the morning and Wet Bob's kit after luncheon, until it was time for her (heavily supervised) shower before tea.

PART THREE

Ancient and Modern:
Two Journeys in the Levant

March, 1962

I gazed down the road towards Smyrna and then back towards Ephesus: pitted with potholes, yellow in the centre, with brown stripes (our tyre tracks) at the edges, it wound over the plain like a rowing scarf discarded on the changing-room floor.

'Why,' I said to O., 'did you not let us fill up with petrol before leaving Ephesus?'

'Because there was only that filthy Turkish stuff. My nice car deserves Shell.'

This was in the spring of 1962, when petrol stations in Turkey were rare and unaccommodating. We had brought the car over from Cyprus to Mersin in a ferry, and were now making north towards Constantinople and the Greek border; ultimate destination, Dover.

'And now,' I said, 'your nice car has an empty tank. There will be no petrol pumps before Smyrna –'

' – Ismir, they call it now –'

' – And you knew very well that we could never make Smyrna from Ephesus –'

' – Ephevs –'

' – On the bare gallon we had in the tank. So why, oh WHY, did you not let us take on petrol, *any kind of petrol*, in Ephesus?'

'I had respect for the engine of my lovely new Morris Traveller and faith in Allah.'

A Turkish AA van stopped beside us and offered to sell us enough petrol to get to Smyrna.

'You see. Allah is mighty. It is probably,' said O., 'the only AA van in Turkey. So say thank you nicely to Allah. As it happened,

I spotted it behind us in Ephevs. About a furlong behind us. You were too busy panicking over the petrol gauge to notice. So I decided to go on, knowing that it would be following us – there is, after all, only the one road and anxious to see what sort of fool you would make of yourself after we ran out and before the rescue van caught up. I accelerated quite a bit, as you may have noticed, to give you ample opportunity. I never saw such hysteria. Your turn to drive and for Allah's sake mind the potholes.'

April, 1988

'I never play chess for money,' said O. in my room at the Hôtel de Château de Montreuil, in the spring of 1988, just over twenty-six years after the scene on the road to Smyrna.

This time we were going the other way: we had just left Dover and were bound, by a circuitous route of my devising, for the Languedoc, the Italian Lakes, Yugoslavia, Roumeli and ultimately Mount Olympus, where we were going to look for any traces that might linger of the Pagan gods (a jokey, journalistic venture, like the round-about route of my devising). After Olympus – well, we would see.

'I never play chess for money,' repeated O.

'But O. You challenged me. Without any prompting on my part, you challenged me, both orally and in writing, to a series of matches, one every day during our entire trip, at a stake of one hundred guineas a match. Both orally and in writing I accepted the challenge. Both orally and in writing you accepted, so to speak, my acceptance. You cannot back out now.

O. had got cold feet. He had remembered, late one night, that some years before he had beaten me with fool's mate. So the challenge had been issued, accepted and confirmed. Later, he had remembered – or rather, had been reminded by an officious cousin – that I had been drunk when he fool's-mated me and that my brother had played chess for Charterhouse from the age

56

of fourteen. He had done his careful little sums and had changed his careful little mind, and now, 'I never play chess for money,' said O. 'Nobody does; it is simply not done.'

He started stroking and apparently elongating his huge, hooky nose until it nearly mated with the dent in his chin.

'I am simply holding you to your own spontaneous challenge,' I said. 'That is all.'

'I never play chess for money; *that* is all. But since I have been at great pains to procure a set made of wood and not of plastic, we shall at least play.'

O. stroked the two tenuous strands on his shining head. Having drawn the white pieces, he played king's pawn to K3. A thoroughly annoying start.

March, 1962

As we neared Smyrna, the potholes became even more numerous and discommoding. Being displeased with O. I made no attempt to avoid them. O. jutted his nose and remained silent…until eventually, 'In Ismir,' he said, 'there is a garage that undertakes serious repair work on Morrises.'

'What sort of work?'

'Checking the chassis, in this instance, to see what damage has been done in these potholes.'

'There's no avoiding them.'

'You could drive a little slower.'

'I don't want to spend the rest of the day getting to Smyrna,' I said.

'Then you'll have to spend the rest of the day hanging about there while the chassis is checked.'

'But we badly want to get on.'

'Not until the chassis is checked,' O. said. 'I value my nice new Morris Traveller even if you don't. Quite apart from anything else, I wangled it tax free because I was a soldier serving in Cyprus. I shan't get a chance like that again. So if you don't mind, old bean, we'll have the chassis checked at that garage in Ismir – as you ought to be calling it. I know you favour the Greeks, but this is nevertheless a Turkish country and has been for half a millennium.'

The garage was in a slum towards the north of Smyrna. Or rather, it adjoined the slum on one side and a river marsh on the other. There was a certain melancholy romance about the marsh and the wooden warehouses on the other side of the slow, smelly river, which was just beginning to swell into an estuary; but any pleasure which one might have derived from this was exhausted long before the five-hour examination of the chassis had been completed.

'Go for a walk,' said O.

'There's nowhere except that heaving slum.'

'Then sit down and read a book.'

'There's nowhere clean to sit down – except the car and that's up on the hoist.'

'Then *sois philosophe*, old bean, as you yourself are always recommending to others.'

A sullen Turkish mechanic dragged O. away to look at an imaginary warp in the rear axle.

'Please,' I almost sobbed, 'please can we leave this place and get on?'

'When the chassis has been duly passed,' said O., 'by this obliging Turkish gentleman. To say nothing, dear bean, of this axle. You shouldn't get into silly tantrums, you see, and go banging in and out of potholes.'

April, 1988

Having paused for some days at Poitiers and Albi to examine basilicas and Toulouse-Lautrec's rude ladies, we pottered along the coast and stopped for a night at Sète.

The Grand Hotel, on the main canal through Sète, has an interior court or atrium, round and above which rise many tiers of narrow balconies along which the bedrooms are approached.

'Funny set-up to be allowed these days,' said O. 'I should have thought the authorities would have been scared of suicides; over the low balustrade on one of the higher balconies and down you go on to this marble floor.'

'The French are too sensible to prevent suicides: as far as they are concerned, if someone wants to die, let him.'

'Could be embarrassing, even so. One is sitting in this court having coffee and cognac, let's say, and down comes some thwarted lover or crooked bankrupt and splashes his brains into one's Delamain VSOP.'

'The possibility does not seem to be putting you off. A thoroughly nice place to sit,' I said, 'suicides or no suicides – '

' – Unless one lands right on top of *one* – '

' – So let's play our game of chess under the lowest balcony. That way we shall be quite safe and command an excellent view of any drama.'

'We shan't,' said O., 'see the actual drop, as they say in the parachute regiment.'

'But we shall have a superb view of what I believe they call the dropping zone,' I said, 'i.e., where the chaps end up. You're already 700 guineas down,' I went on as O. began to set up the board.

'I told you our first night out. I don't play chess for money.'

'And I told you. You can't grease out of a challenge once given and accepted and confirmed. What I will do,' I said, 'if I end the tour still ahead, is cut the guineas to sovereigns. After all, the guinea doesn't exist any more.'

'Nor does the sovereign.'

'Yes, it does. It is habitually used in racing circles,' I said, 'to denote one-pound sterling. And now I come to think of it, the guinea is still used as a unit in auctions on racecourses. Which being so, we may revert to guineas without being guilty of anachronism. So: you are now down 700 guineas.'

'What I can't stand,' said O. as we settled down to play over two liberal balloons of Marc de Provence, is your creepy-crawly use of pawns.'

He started one of his tremendous queen and bishop movements. I waited. The moment came. I forced him to swap queens and was now left three pawns ahead.

'Why can't you play like a man?' said O. 'Only a funk swaps queens.'

'Your queen is like an unexploded bomb; one must defuse it as quickly as possible. Check.'

'So now you're going to swap castles as well.'

'Of course. I have pawn superiority, you see.'

'How loathsome. You're a disgrace to the regiment.'

'I always was. So were you. But one might just drink to it – '

' – Although it no longer exists – '

' – So here's to the Fifty-Third,' I said, sipping my Marc de Provence. 'Check again.'

'Swapping bishops now?'

'Everything. So that I can get one of my three gash pawns through and promote it to queen. You haven't yet drunk to the regiment.'

'Here's to the Fifty-Third of Foot,' said O. He swallowed, as I knew he would for this particular toast, his entire glass of Marc, thus doing himself honour and depriving himself of his wits. I was now 800 guineas ahead, with at least a dozen games to go between Sète and Mount Olympus, to look no further than that.

March, 1962

'Troy,' said O., 'cannot be reached today.'

'Nonsense,' I said. 'Here it is on the map. Bergamos equals Pergamos equals Pergamum equals a citadel equals the citadel of

Troy, which is often called Pergamum or Pergama in the epics of Virgil and Homer.'

'Have it your own way,' said O. 'You're the classical scholar. By all means let us go to Bergamos and call it Troy.'

We set out, bitter and bedraggled, from the slum of Smyrna where we had passed one of the most wretched nights in the history of the world.

'Please, O.,' I said. 'You have had your revenge. Under pretence of having to rectify this car, you have made me spend an afternoon in a river marsh, an evening in a thieves' drinking den and a night in a tenth-rate brothel. Now let me enjoy my vision of Troy in peace.'

'Not much sea about,' said O. as we drew near to Bergamos some hours later. 'Surely Troy was on the sea.'

'In nearly 3,000 years the sea,' I said, 'has receded.'

'Funny thing,' O. said as we drove up to the citadel. 'It's all of a piece. I thought Troy was in layers – you know, Third Millennium BC, Second Mil BC, Homer's Troy that was razed to the ground and so on. *This* is just run-of-the-mill Roman stuff.'

'There was a Roman Troy.'

'And about fourteen others,' O. said. 'No sign of any of 'em here. Besides, according to the book you can't drive up the citadel of Troy – in so far as there *is* a citadel still – you have to park outside the wall underneath. Now here we have a spanking great car park complete with shopping centre. The book says that all shops and restaurants at Troy are, like the car park, under the wall.'

'The book is out of date. Stop trying to upset me. I was remembering the passage in the *Iliad* in which Helen walks on the walls of Troy and wonders why her two brothers aren't among the leaders of the Greeks on the plain beneath.'

'Why weren't they?'

'Dead – out of shame at her behaviour.'

'Well, here there isn't a plain. There're only more hills.'

'Scholars,' I said, 'have always been uncertain about the exact nature of the terrain.'

'Look,' said O. 'Pergamum may mean a citadel and may have been used by poets as a name for Troy; but Troy itself is in the middle of a military zone, so the AA instructions tell me here, and many miles to the north. To enter it you have to have a special permit. So we *are* somewhere different.'

'Don't rub it in.'

'Even I,' said O., 'who am not a scholar, know that certain words, like *pergamum*, meaning a height, or *purgos*, meaning a tower, or *potamos* meaning a river, are used to designate three-quarters of the towns that actually have heights, towers or rivers. So why you should imagine that this *pergamum* or height is Troy, any more than any of the 4,000 other *pergamums* in the Balkans, is quite beyond me.'

'I said, don't rub it in. I was over eager.'

'Yes. That's the trouble with you romantics. You see Troy or Atlantis or what not whenever and wherever it suits you, just because you're in the mood.'

'Same trouble with you soldiers. You disregard any factors that don't suit your own pet personal plan.'

'Support that assertion.'

'Von Clausewitz is with me for one. He maintains that generals, like scholars, live in a dreamworld where everything is ordered as they desire. And if it turns out not to be, they start whining: either someone has lied to them, or betrayed them, or simply been inefficient. It's never *their* fault.'

'Just because you were more or less booted out of the army,' said O., 'is no reason to vilify the profession. My profession.'

'At least I'm ready to admit I was wrong about Troy.'

'You hadn't much choice.'

'Can we get back on the road to it?'

'Oh yes. The office which issues permits, the AA instructions say, is open between ten and twelve in the morning. Because we've spent this afternoon faffing about here, we shan't get there till well after noon tomorrow. Too late.'

'And the next day?'

'Monday. Closing day at the office. No time to hang around till the day after. You'll have to miss Helen's wall, I'm afraid. Serves you right for being rude about soldiers.'

April, 1988

In the gardens of the Albergo Catullo in Sirmione (Sirmio) there was, predictably, a bust of Catullus, with a potted biography on the pedestal and some of his lines in praise of the place.

'He was born here then?' said O. 'And the Hotel is doubling its charges on that account?'

'He was born in Verona,' I said, 'and spent most of his time in Rome. But the family had an estate near here.'

'I see. Absentee landlords. But this Hotel still feels entitled to push its charges up to the moon on the strength of his name and a botched nineteenth-century bust of the fellow?'

'This Hotel's charges are high,' I said, having chosen it myself, 'because it is near the shore of a delectable lake and built on what Catullus calls the "Jewel of all islands and near islands". By which he means the peninsula of Sirmio.'

'So I assumed. It says here under the bust that your man Catullus was a poet *and* a soldier.'

'He was an ADC or an equerry to a colonial governor.'

'*That* sort of soldier,' said O. 'The sort that dies in bed.'

'He certainly died young. Thirty-three at the most. He felt seedy, took to his bed, wrote a melancholy little poem to a friend – and then died.'

'What of? Excess? He does have a reputation for doing it rather a lot.'

'Not necessarily of that. People did die young in those days. The Romans were pretty hygienic as people go – then or now

– but their medicine was still elementary. Almost any infection could carry you off.'

O. looked out over Catullus' lake, surveyed the motels and caravan sites that lay beside it.

'He wouldn't have cared for those,' O. said. 'How often did he come here? If it had been mine, this estate, I'd have come very often – even these days with all these beastly trippers.'

'We only know of one visit,' I said. 'He came here on his way back from the Troad, after doing his stint with the colonial governor-general in Asia Minor. While in the Troad he'd visited the tomb of his brother and had been much affected. So on his way home he'd come to see the old family villa on the estate near Sirmio.'

'But he didn't stay? He went back to Rome?'

'Yes.'

'I thought so,' said O. 'A city man, obviously. Happy to take a cushy job on a governor's staff for a time, but then sliding out as quick as he could and coming home early.'

'There is certainly a poem which suggests that he got very fed up with Asia Minor. A poem about the return of spring…which seems to be making him homesick.'

'That fits. He gets bored with the service and its discomforts, turns for home, goes to see his brother's grave near Troy on his way to a convenient port…'

'And then comes here to Sirmio.'

'The renegade soldier,' said O.

'The poet,' said I.

'What did he write of? Wasn't there enough in Asia Minor? Or here at Sirmio? Why did he want to go back to Rome? He betrayed the service to come back to Italy and then spurned his family place to return to Rome. What was the matter with him?'

'Love, I suppose… He had broken with all his lovers, who had in one way or other been false to him. Perhaps he was hoping for a new one. You asked me just now what he wrote about. He wrote about the inception of love, its inevitable decay and then its renewal with a different lover. There is a long and haunting poem about the desertion of Ariadne on the seashore by the treacherous Theseus and her tremendous reawakening, just as she is about to die, by Bacchus, who is processing with his followers in triumph.'

'So you think Catullus hoped for some such reawakening if he returned to Rome? Or simply hankered for the superior whorehouses which are on offer in a capital city?'

'The poems suggest both. They also suggest that he was in any case betrayed again:

Malest, Cornifici, tuo Catullo...
It goes ill, Cornificus, with your Catullus;
It goes ill and yet more cruel as each hour drags by.
Why could you not have come to comfort him?
(So light a task.) Why treat your lover so?'

'That is the poem which you told me he wrote on his deathbed?'

'So they say.'

'People who let down the service,' said O., 'even if they are famous and talented poets, must expect to be served in kind. Why should they be let off? A good thing they're not, if you come to think of it: they make such touching poetry out of being forsaken.'

'I suppose so. And when all is said, even after this last betrayal, Catullus did find a new lover, the most comforting and dependable of all.'

March, 1962

We both hated Istanbul from the moment we reached it, after a long slog over the dreary roads of the Troad. What could have caused this hatred is not hard to tell. It was the capacity of the city for wilfully expunging the charm and brilliance of all the most beautiful and wondrous sights which it had to offer.

For example: coming from the East, we had to cross the Bosporus to reach the main part of the city, in which we had reservations in a hotel called the Divan. The crossing of the Bosporus, for the first time, should surely have been an unforgettable experience; and so it was, quite unforgettable for the sheer squalor of the ferry, the rapacity of the officials, the stink of the crowd, the filth of the waters and the utter ineptness of the arrangements for the embarkation and disembarkation of the car and ourselves. In order to make work for themselves and inconvenience for the passengers, the Turks insisted that the co-driver of the car should get out and board the ferry separately and (as I remember) should pay twice – once as a car passenger and once as a passenger on foot.

Or again: we had deliberately chosen the Divan because it was supposed to be a hotel of class and comfort in which we could (we thought) thoroughly service ourselves, our belongings and the car after the trek through Bithynia and before traversing the desolate reaches of Thrace to Adrianople and Thessalonika. And to be sure, the Divan did everything it could, for not unreasonable charges, to assist us: it fed and soothed us, guided us to Agia Sophia and the Blue Mosque, attended to our laundry and arranged for the inspection of O.'s car. Even the Divan, however, could not do much to mitigate the malignance of Turkish bureaucracy. Whatever one wished to do or have done, there was first a little matter of what the Turks called 'formalities', pronounced 'formaleeties'.

'First, little formaleety. You have insurance for car?'

'Yes. The certificate was checked when docked at Iskenderu and again when we drove ashore at Mersin.'

'Ah. But now is Istanbul. Special insurance between Istanbul and Adrianople.'

'Why?'

'Why? Because is frontier contry with Greece, that is why. Secureety. Special insurance, special permission needed.'

'It says nothing about that in the *AA Instructions and Route* which we have here.'

'New regulations.'

'But look here. You are a *garage*, recommended by the Divan Hotel to service this car. What have all these insurances and permissions to do with you?'

'We must show list of work done to Transport Office. They say, "English car. Why do you not report before you begin work? All foreign cars you must report." '

'So what do we do?'

'You go to Transport Office and do formaleeties. Then come back here with certificate and we do servicing.'

'Suppose we just forget about the servicing and take the car away?'

'Nevertheless, we have seen car and must report to the Transport Office. You will be stopped on the road.'

'Is there,' said O., 'no...so to speak...short cut?'

'Short cut?'

'Method of...special payment...to avoid delay?'

'But of course. We 'ave insurance certificate and special permission on sale here, on commission, by accredited licence from Transport Office. But more expensive – much more expensive – if you buy here and not at Transport Office.'

'How expensive?'

The manager of the garage named a figure and beamed with avarice. Yet the figure was relatively small; for one of the endearing things about the Turks – indeed, the only endearing thing – is their sheer incompetence. They get their schemes and scales wrong because they are too idle to do their homework, nor did all the nagging and officiousness of Ataturk suffice to get them up to the mark. In this instance, despite their cupidity, the garage manager and the junior officials with whom he was in league had simply miscalculated the amount of money which

O. and I could afford to save ourselves trouble and had put their demand far too low. After much pretended agony, protest and supplication (it is wonderful how cunning you become after only a few days in Turkey) O. and I eventually consented to pay their price. The garage manager took our cash, issued the (supposedly) required papers and promised (not with absolute falsity as it turned out) that a good job would be made of O.'s Morris Traveller.

All this kind of thing, making for hatred and contempt of the Turks, forged a strong temporary bond between O. and myself. Forgotten, for the time being, were the reciprocal resentments in which the journey had hitherto abounded.

'I suppose it's much the same in all big cities except in Britain and the Colonies,' said O. (We still called them 'Colonies' then.) 'But I must say, the people do not compare favourably with the Turks in Cyprus...who are much more honest and manly than the Greeks there.'

'They could hardly not be, if one considers the Cypriot Greeks. Taxi drivers and pimps.'

'Ah. Pimps. I hear there is an interesting walled brothel quarter here that has survived from before the Fourth Crusade. Very much your sort of thing...a Romanesque red-light district. Rather a romantic notion don't you think?'

Most of the clientele of the romantic and Romanesque red-light district seemed to be queuing, not to get into the girls' quarters, but in order to be allowed to pay for a period of between thirty seconds and three minutes at the window (a chink was always left in the curtain) or the keyhole of the downstairs accommodation.

'I wonder they don't provide ladders,' O. said. 'Then they could charge for upstairs viewing as well.'

I laughed.

'Excuse me,' said a voice behind us in English, 'but the peoples who come here are taking their − activities − very seriously. They are not wishing to be laughed at.'

We turned and saw the garage manager.

'I am 'ere to tell you your car will be ready tomorrow. Some time before the evening.'

'Thank you. How did you know we were here?'

'The receptionist at your hotel heard your discussion of the architecture 'ere. He told me, when I came to ask for you. He has also, of course, notified the police.'

'For our protection?' said O. 'Jolly civil, I call that.'

'No. Not for your protection. As foreigners you need a police permission to visit this place.'

'Oh. We didn't know.'

'Is quite all right. The receptionist is empowered by the police to issue the permissions. He give them to me to bring to you.'

He named a sum something under one-pound sterling for each 'persmission'. We paid. He withdrew. So, after a little while longer of watching the frenzied queuing and requeuing, did we.

'Even when they had their eyes glued to the apertures,' said O., 'they did not appear to be...exciting themselves. What is the point of the exercise?'

'Perhaps they remember what they saw for later recall in private. I expect public onanism is illegal. Or makes for loss of face.'

'How much do you suppose they charge,' O. said, 'if you actually go inside?'

'I've no idea. We haven't *seen* anyone actually go in yet. Perhaps the girls just pose for the keyhole artists. Or perhaps all the chaps are too scared of the pox actually to do it.'

'Shall we stand in the queue and find out what does go on inside?'

'No,' I said. 'We should probably need another permission... I have enjoyed driving through Turkey; but I loathe the Byzantines more than I can say.'

'Byzantines?'

'Istanbul was Constantinople until the Turks came and Byzantium until Constantine came.'

'Surely the old Byzantines must have been more attractive than this crew?'

'Far worse. Most of them were Greek, you see.'

'Are we really sure that the Greeks are nastier than the Turks?'

'Yes. They are more perspicacious, for one thing, and would never put such a low price on corruption.'

'In a day or two,' said O., 'we shall be in Greece. Do you mean to tell me that we shall have to go on buying these sort of certificates and permissions, and at far higher prices?'

'Not exactly. It's a difference of emphasis. The Turks, as you will have noticed, at least those in Istanbul, have a genius for making pleasant things horrid by mismanagement and trivial venality. The Greeks, on the other hand, have a genius for making horrid things appear pleasant by sheer sleight of hand and then charging the maximum the market will bear, which they are very shrewd at calculating.'

'Concrete examples, please.'

'For Turkish behaviour, that brothel quarter. Exquisite surroundings, ruined by those sordid queues of *voyeurs* and the infliction of irritating charges for nothing.'

'And of Greek behaviour?'

'Let's say…the ruins of Knossos. A few ugly and garishly painted columns, and a lot of boring and narrow concrete corridors. But call it 'a labyrinth', as the Cretans do, and say that a man-eating monster lives at the centre of it, a monster begotten by a bull on a queen in *oestrus* who disguised herself as a cow – say something like that and you can charge what you will for admittance.'

April, 1988

As we drove from Sirmione to Trieste and then south towards
Split, O. was still expressing annoyance with Catullus – and with
me for having been on his side.

'You were the same when you were with the battalion,' he
said. 'Arty and unreliable.'

It was clearly essential to focus his disapproval of me on a
new topic; and with this in view I turned off the coast road on
to a bridge which crossed a canal and brought us to the old
Venetian offshore island of Trogir. I then sat him down in a café
behind the cathedral, on a quayside which faced over a small
bay.

He took to the place, as everyone does at first. He drank his
beer and enjoyed his view, then walked about, admired the
loggia, the campanile, the façade and narthex of the cathedral,
the Old Palace and the New, and the promenade with the view
of Čiovo.

'Very agreeable,' said O. at length. 'Yet there is something not
right about this engaging little town; something unwholesome,
something sinister, something almost macabre.'

'Right,' I said. 'What?'

'When one looks carefully at the little garden at the north
end of the promenade, one sees that it is strewn with every kind
of rubbish from bottles to excrement. But of course that is
nothing out of the way anywhere these days.'

'So try again,' I said.

'When one looks across the strip of water to the island over
there, one sees that one-third of the pine forest is dying. But
neither is that unusual.'

'So try once more,' I said. 'Observation test. Look here, in this
little square. A charming piazza. There is the post office in a
building of the seventeenth century, and opposite the post
office is a house which the Blue Guide tells us is late
Romanesque of the thirteenth century. People are going in and

out of the post office; a female servant is brushing the threshold of the house. All very nice and normal. And yet, as you remark, there is something not right, something rather perverse about it all. Even something monstrous.'

'I see children, ordinary, healthy children. So there cannot be any kind of serious pestilence here, despite the condition of the gardens and those diseased trees over the bay.'

'Yes,' I said. 'Children from toddlers to early adolescents. Whom else can you see?'

'I can see…a number of elderly people. Well set up and quite spruce for their age.'

'Exactly. Further confirmation – or so one would have thought – that there is nothing much wrong with the air or the food or the drains. No kind of pestilence, as you put it. So. Look yet again and tell me what is the omission here.'

'There appears to be nobody,' said O. at last, 'between the ages of fifteen and fifty.'

'Correct. If you are born in Trogir you leave at fifteen and you do not return, except for brief and specially sanctioned visits, until you are fifty.'

'Then how are all these children here? I mean, if there are no mature men or women in the town, how are children born in the place for a start?'

'The parents come back here briefly for the birth of their children. After two months, they leave them behind with the grandparents and visit them perhaps once a year thereafter.'

'But surely…the mothers at least must hate that?'

'The mothers are from Trogir. So are the fathers. Both know the rules.'

'Do you mean to tell me…that although they all leave this place when they are fifteen…they marry only fellow Trogirians? Where do they all go, for Christ's sake? Surely not all to the same place?'

'No. They go south to Split, to Dubrovnik, right down to Ulcinj. They go north to Zadar, Rijeka, Trieste and Venice. But wherever they go there will be those from Trogir who accompany them, who have come there before them, and who will come soon after them. Among these they marry – among these only.'

'Why…these only?'

'Because no one else will marry them. Everyone knows that they come from Trogir to avoid the curse.'

'For heaven's sake.'

'In the eleventh century,' I told him, 'the Saracens were here. They either occupied the town or made an almost continuous series of raids on it. When they left, they abducted, for sale as slaves, every adult between the ages of fifteen or fifty, except for the diseased or the decrepit.'

'Why didn't they take the younger children? Young children were thought to make very appetising slaves.'

'Usually, yes. In this case the Saracens were in a hurry to get out, as strong forces from Venice were on the way to repel them. They had very limited room on their ships. There was a long hard voyage before them. Relays of rowers would be needed. They chose the able-bodied rather than the appetising.'

'In those days nobody over forty would have been much good for anything. And yet you say they took everyone between fifteen and fifty.'

'Then as now the inhabitants of Trogir were very healthy. The Saracens regard elder people as repositories of knowledge and experience. The men of Trogir, in those days, were highly skilled artisans, the women excellent cooks.'

The post office closed its doors. Evening is coming, I thought. But so long as one was gone before dark…

'The incident was nothing much out of the ordinary for the era in which it occurred,' I went on, 'and nobody would have thought much more about it, had it not been for what happened to the Saracen ships.'

'And what was that?'

'They sailed south down the Adriatic – and vanished entirely. Not uncommon in the Mediterranean, then or since. A sudden freak storm – whirlwinds and whirlpools, fatal to small craft. So even then nothing much would have been thought about it…had not the inhabitants of Othoni, north-west of Corfu, reported an invasion of "ghost-people", who arrived once a year in Saracen "ghost-ships", encamped on the shore of one night, during which they feasted off any livestock or human beings to be found, and by the following dawn had disappeared, leaving only large piles of bones behind them.

'This tale, of course, was an obvious variant of Corfiot tradition about vampires (who devour flesh rather than suck blood) and was accorded scant respect until, five centuries later, the Corfiot Count Cuccumeli, having gone to Othoni to collect rent due to him in salt fish and having been delayed over night by inclement weather, himself witnessed one of these sudden "ghost-invasions" (which came from nowhere out of the storm) and narrowly avoided, if we are to believe his journal, being consumed at the revenants' banquet.'

'So,' said O., 'this little town is responsible for providing much of the "manpower" in a vampire fleet that for hundreds of years has been preying on the cattle and the peasants of Othoni.'

'They are almost all fisher-folk. Cattle is scarce. There are a few sheep.'

'You would have thought the phantom fleet – '

' – In the circumstances, "phantom" is not quite the right word – '

' – You would have thought that the commanders of this mysterious fleet would have tried more prosperous islands or coasts than some wretched piece of pumice off Corfu. Corfu itself would surely be an inviting target?'

'These…mariners…shun publicity. Apart from Othoni, they have been reported only from almost deserted sections of the coasts of Albania and the Mani, and from two or three tiny Aegean and Tyrrhene islets.'

O. walked back on to the promenade and took a long look at the decaying pine trees of Čiovo.

'I suppose,' he said, 'that the custom of leaving this island at fifteen and not returning for thirty-five years is based on atavistic fears of being abducted by this pirate fleet (which is known to be still at large) for the slave market, and then being transformed, forever, into a sea-roving vampire. All Trogirians depart to avoid this fate – the curse of their ancestors. Wherever they go they are recognised as fugitives from a curse and no one will marry with them. Meanwhile, their children are deposited with the grandparents here in Trogir. Why don't the parents keep these children with them, in Split or Dubrovnik or wherever?'

'Because anywhere other than in Trogir they would be slaughtered – as the infected and infectious offspring of a vampire race. The adults of Trogir flee the town in order to avoid being abducted and turned into vampires; but the sad irony is that they are in any case widely assumed to have inherited, already, the taint of their forebears. Not only will other people not marry with them: they shun them altogether with fear and hatred and would certainly murder them if given a safe opportunity. From which it follows that their weak and innocent children would be constantly in danger, and so must be born and brought up in Trogir itself.'

'Who employs them – when they are old enough to leave Trogir? Who employs the descendants of a vampire race?'

'They are in great demand for hard labour in field and factory. There is a legend, in this part of the world, that if you feed a vampire well on red meat he will repay you with prodigiously hard work. They are given a wide berth by the superstitious, as I say, but they are not short of employment.'

'And then at fifty, when they are safe from the fleet, should it return, they go back to Trogir?'

'Yes. They are prudent and save money. They will live comfortably from fifty to their death, usually at an advanced age, pleasantly occupied by the care of their children's children and amply subsidised for this by the absent and hard-working parents.'

'I see,' said O. 'And although they have such a beautiful town to live in, they cannot be bothered to clear up the public gardens or cut down polluted trees in the area?'

'They like the place to appear run down. If you have noticed, there are some architectural features which, though beautiful, badly need restoring. They will never be restored. Ruin and decay help to deaden any yearning that the Saracens or their own ancestors may have to return in their vampire ships. The departure of all potential victims or recruits at maturity does the rest. The rules are very strict. Boys and girls must be gone a good month before their fifteenth birthdays. Returns to give birth or visit children are carefully limited in number and extent.'

'And so the vampire ships have not come back to Trogir?'

'Not yet. Though one never knows…'

'Where were they last heard of?'

'In Anti-Paxos, a very spare area of depredation, some seven years ago.'

'Seven years? The vampires must be ill-nourished by now,' conjectured O.

'Yes. Time to leave, don't you think?'

O. shivered. Despite tiffs and tantrums earlier in our journey, we were now united in horror of Trogir.

'The car,' said O., 'the car. You were driving when we got here. Can you find it by that canal? You have the key safe? I think it is already getting dark.'

'We have a minute or two,' I said, as the big red sun hovered over the living dead pines of Čiovo.

March, 1962

'To be or not to be,' I spouted from the floor of the theatre at Delphi, 'that is the question.'

O. gave the thumbs up sign from the top tier of seats.

'Clear as Henry Irving, old bean,' he called.

'Very proper. This theatre is sacred to Apollo, god of light, prophecy and poetry. Apollo was both exact and exacting. He expected things to be accurately calculated and constructed, and to work without interruption, so smoothly as never even to be noticed. Hence the perfection of the acoustics here. Apollo had a very masculine sense of priorities.'

'What on earth did you mean by that?'

'Apollo represents the male principle: he imposes form on the formless female. As the sun, he quickens the earth; as the god of truth, he destroyed the evil monster that guarded the dark shrine of the earth-mother here, and set up a new shrine of foresight and enlightenment.'

'What's all this got to do with anything?' said O. crossly.

'I was just trying to explain what goes on here.'

'I'm sick of the sound of Apollo. Apollo this and Apollo that ever since we arrived in Greece. All the way through that superb Vale of Tempe I had to listen to your lecture about how it was sacred to Apollo.'

'So it was. It was there that he plucked the laurel branch which he brought to Delphi – '

' – I don't quarrel with your version of the legend, though there are probably fifty others. What I'm complaining about,' said O., 'is your insistence on Apollo's male superiority. The earth-mother, according to you, is at best a blind and shapeless womb, which is graciously impregnated by Apollo, and at worst a principle of evil, which he destroys. To me the earth-mother is the giver of fertility – '

' – Only when first serviced by Apollo – '

' – And certainly not a principle of evil.'

'Not so much of evil as of muddle and stupidity and mess. The primitive inhabitants of Greece worshipped the female as the "one that brought forth". Later invaders from the North pointed out that the female just lay about bringing forth nothing until quickened and shaped by the male. Matriarchy was then abandoned – not before time – and the king and the male recognised as the ultimate provider of life. That is what I meant by saying that Apollo has a male sense of priorities. He knows that light and intelligence and poetry (the language of revelation) are essential, along with precision and energy, to quicken the female womb into any kind of satisfactory production.'

'In other words, women are cattle?' said O. furiously.

'What on earth has come over you? You're carrying on like a suffragette.'

We walked away from the theatre along the track towards the Treasuries.

'You too had a mother, I suppose,' said O. at length.

'Yes. And so did you. And I have never heard you say a single pleasant thing about her. She is an old hag, an ignorant biddie, a gormless cow, a clucking hen, a possessive harpy – '

' – Stop. In a few days' time it is her birthday.'

'What's that got to do with it?'

We left the precinct, walked down the road and clambered into O.'s Morris Traveller.

'One's mother's birthday,' said O., as he started the Morris, 'is an occasion for reverence.'

'What is the matter with you?'

'One owes one's being to one's mother, just as the people of the world owe their existence to the earth-mother. And no amount of your clever clever talk about Apollo the god of truth and poetry is going to alter that. It's all part of your fundamental artiness and unreliability.'

We drew up by the Xenia, ordered tea on the balcony and sat looking out over the great gorge of Delphi, where the eagles hover and wheel and the mountains march against the never-resting sea. Though for the moment we were quiet, we were both sulking and I could not for the life of me conceive what had induced O.'s sudden and ludicrous feminist fervour. The truce consequent upon our shared and contemptuous relish of Turkish behaviour in Istanbul was now at an end.

April, 1988

At about the same time of the day and pretty well the same time of the year, we sat in precisely the same place, over quarter of a century later, having driven, this time, down and round the coast from Igoumenitsa, which we had reached by boat from Dubrovnik.

'At least,' said O., 'there are no Americans this time.'

'They all go to the new hotel up the hill.'

'Thank God for the new hotel.'

'This one doesn't take American Express Cards. None of the Xenias seems to.'

'When we were here in 1962 we hadn't even heard of credit cards. We seemed to get on well enough without them.'

'It was a horrible bore having to find cash for everything... I suppose,' I said, 'that we'd better go and look at the site.'

'Will it have changed since we were here last time?'

'I believe they've done some more excavating and improved the footpaths. And multiplied the charge for admission by about 2,000 per cent.'

'Let's not go then,' said O. 'After all, the whole point of Delphi is in this gorge.'

'It's rather slack to come to Delphi and not to visit the shrine. It shows a distinct lack of respect for Apollo. He is, you know, a vital god to a writer.'

'Yes,' said O. 'I remember your being keen about Apollo. The male principle, you said. The male that gives meaning to a formless female and turns it into a mother.'

'And you got so cross because it was near your mother's birthday.'

'I can't imagine what came over me,' said O., 'being so aggressive towards you – in defence of my mother, of all people.'

'Ah well. *De mortuis.* I think I shall have to go at least to the museum,' I said. 'They now have a marble head of Timandros.'

'What's the attraction about him?'

'He was an Athenian captured in Sicily when the invading army was defeated. He was sold as a slave but manumitted by the Syracusans who purchased him because he was able to quote, and then write down for them, long passages from Euripides and other poets. When he had written all he could remember, they let him go out of gratitude. A pleasing tale.'

'Why have they got a head of him here?'

'Because he came here, on his way home to Athens, to thank Apollo, as the god of poetry, for his freedom. While he was here, he was spotted by a relative, a distant cousin, who had come to consult the oracle about how to bring about the release from Sicily of his son. When this chap saw Timandros, he asked him how he got away and Timandros told him. The cousin came out wild with anger, accusing Timandros of being sly and unmanly and greasing his way out of trouble instead of escaping honourably, as a soldier should. His son, said Timandros' cousin, had had no truck with poetry and such during the war, he had simply done his duty as an officer – and now where was his reward? He was still stuck in the quarries of Syracuse, while the glib, shirking, effeminate, sycophantic Timandros was on his way home to Athens. Timandros rebuked his cousin for speaking ill of poetry and its devotees in the shrine of Apollo, whereupon the cousin lost his temper and killed him dead with a rock there and then, and on holy ground. The thing became a *cause célèbre* and Timandros emerged as a martyr for the honour of poetry. Hence his place in the museum here.'

O.'s face darkened.

'Typical of you to approve of that story,' he said. 'I'm for Timandros' cousin's son, who stayed with his men in the quarries, while Timandros just deserted the army and went home.'

'But Timandros no longer had anything to do with the army. He was a manumitted slave.'

'Precisely. Manumitted. The moment he was free, he should have enquired after his unit and rejoined it in the quarries or wherever it was.'

'No one volunteered to go into the quarries. Have you read Thucydides' account?'

'Of course not,' said O. 'I know the story, but when would I have had time to squander reading Thucydides? I've just been a simple soldier all these years, like Timandros' second cousin or whatever he was.'

'You did retire a few years ago...'

'That's not to say I had time to read Thucydides or any of this bloody poetry you keep going on about. What with keeping things together, and shooting and fishing and going to see my mother's relations in America...'

'All right,' I said. 'It's not a crime not to read Thucydides.'

'*You* almost think it is. At any rate you think you're superior because you have. All fancy wind and arty piss, you are: no wonder you didn't make a decent enough soldier to stay in the regiment.'

The truce formed in Trogir was clearly over. For the second time in twenty-six years I had made the wrong remark in Delphi (speaking off the top of my head and meaning no harm to anybody) and had blown a dangerous breach in what had seemed, only a few minutes previously, a grateful and secure peace.

March, 1962

From Delphi we took a ferry to the south coast of the Corinthian Gulf, drove next to Patras and embarked for Corfu. Here we were to stay two days and nights before catching another boat on to Brindisi.

'Some say this island was once ruled by a queen,' I said to O. at Palaiokastritsa as we inspected the supposed site of King Alcinous' Palace. 'Certainly Odysseus was required to make obeisance to her before he did to the King.'

'Don't try to softsoap me. You've made your views on the inferiority of women and the unimportance of motherhood most painfully clear.'

'What you need is exercise,' I said. 'We'll climb up to the Castrum Sancti Angeli.'

'What's that in plain English?'

'A castle on a cliff.'

I persuaded him to drive us a mile or two north of Palaiokastritsa to Lakones, near which a mule path ascends the west side of a steep, narrow valley to the Angelo Kastro.

'Built by the despot of the Epirus between 1214 and 1260,' I explained as we climbed, 'to give early warning of pirates or invaders.'

We rounded the last bend of the mule track and started up a steep flight of steps.

'This had better be worth it,' puffed O.

'Come, come. Where's all that military fitness you're always boasting about? There's a graveyard at the top where we can leave you if the climb proves too much.'

'Who ever heard of a graveyard in a look-out post?'

'There was a captain and a troop of soldiers. The mortality rate was high in those days and the summer weather, then as now, very hot.'

And graveyard there was: a few anonymous sarcophagi, half concealed by earth and brambles, near the entrance of a tiny

82

chapel. There was also, when we mounted a hillock west of the chapel, a view: a mighty seascape to the West with a coastline (cliff alternating with dune and sand) to North and South; the twin harbours of Homer's Phaeacia and the Gardens of Alcinous; the Scherian ship which Poseidon had turned to stone as a punishment for its misuse on his waters; and the beach of Ermones (hidden by low hills but clearly marked by the estuary which breached them) where Odysseus was washed ashore after many days adrift on the ocean.

'He went to sleep in the bushes,' I said to O., 'but was woken up by the Princess Nausikaa and her girls...who had come to do the royal laundry and were playing with their ball while waiting for it to dry on the beach. They lost the ball in the river and started squealing. Odysseus came out of the bushes stark naked except for an olive branch, and they all squealed even louder and ran away to hide, except for the Princess, who stood her ground like the daughter of a king, scented something distinguished in this gaunt "stranger from the sea", and invited him back to her father's court in the palace.

'So they all trooped back along the river and came to the harbours and the King's orchards, where Odysseus was told to hide and then follow on alone later, as it would not be proper if he arrived publicly as Nausikaa's pick-up. It is at this stage that the Princess gives him some very curious instructions. When he enters the palace, she says, he will see her father on his throne, which leans against a pillar. On the other side of the pillar, also leaning against it, Odysseus will see her mother, "spinning purple yarn in the light of the fire". Odysseus is to ignore the King and go straight to the Queen, "and cast thy hands about my mother's knees" in order to find favour "and be given passage to thine home".'

'I see,' said O. 'That passage you were talking of the other day – the one which suggests a survival of matriarchy?'

Too late. Carried away with my exegesis of the marvellous legend I had revived the fatal topic.

'And why,' continued O. with some menace, 'do you find the Princess' instructions to be curious?'

'Because even as early as Odysseus, matriarchy was well on the way out. It looks as if this passage must be a survival of some earlier oral tradition.'

'I see. Any instructions instilling proper respect and precedence for the female have to be written off as an accidental intrusion into the text.'

'Really, O. I do *not* understand this new craze of yours for sexual equality – worse, for female superiority.'

'I told you. In a few days my mother –'

'– Will be having her birthday. What about it?'

'At a time like this, a fellow realises what he owes to his mother. I'm afraid I've been a rotten neglectful son. I have disobeyed her and hurt her feelings, and disregarded her wishes and –'

'– And now you're indulging in a fit of guilt. Irrational guilt. Do not forget that I have met your mother,' I cried, looking out over the wine-dark sea, 'and know her to be a mean-minded, empty-headed, jealous, pampered, possessive bitch. All those feelings you have injured were grounded in self-esteem and self-righteousness, all those wishes of hers you have disregarded were the petulant hankerings of an ill-conditioned harridan, all the requests you have disobeyed were the spiteful and tyrannous whimsies of a –'

'– How dare you speak of my mother like this?'

'It's exactly the way you always speak of her.'

'I'm allowed to. She's my mother. In any case I am now repenting, bitterly repenting. When I get home I am going to comfort and cherish her, I am going –'

'– To report to the regimental depot in a matter of days, as ordered before you left Cyprus, so you won't have to spend long on the comforting and cherishing bit.'

'I'm thinking of sending in my papers if she wants me to be with her. My poor, lonely, widowed, neglected mother, how could I have ignored her needs for so long?'

'With the greatest of ease and equanimity. Any other time we've been in a castle like this, you've always said how you wished your mother was with us so that you could push her off the rampart. But now, just because her stupid birthday is coming up – '

' – You don't understand how a decent man's mind works.'

'I understand very well how yours works. The last time you were at home on leave, you balanced a bucket full of coal on the top of the door into her bedroom. If I hadn't taken it down, you'd have been hanged for murder by now.'

'I'm going to make up for all of that,' declared O. 'The first thing I'm going to do is send her a marvellous birthday present.'

'She's got everything she needs. She never spends a ha'-penny on anyone except herself. The last time I came to dinner, she served spaghetti.'

'And that was more than you were worth. As soon as we get to Venice, I'm going to buy her something rich and rare from Fortuny's. There'll be just time to send it to England for the big day – if I express it.'

'And where,' said I, 'are you going to find the money to buy and express presents from Fortuny?'

'From now on I'm going to sleep in the car and save the cost of hotels. And if you've got any friendship in you, you'll do the same, in order to help me pay for this present.'

'I wouldn't give up a single drachma for the sake of your manky old mother.'

'I've a good mind to leave you out here all night. It's *my* car and *I've* got the keys – '

'Well, you can't. Because I bought the ticket at Patras and without it you can't go on to Brindisi.'

'All right. I'll drive you back to the town. But I mean what I say,' said O. 'From now until we get to Venice I am sleeping in no hotels and only eating one meal a day – bread and salami. I am determined to make it up to my mother – and you can sneer as much as you want to.'

'Why should I want to sneer? I'll be the one with the full belly and the warm bed. I shall just pity you, that's all.'

'Keep your pity. I shall have a good conscience and that's the most important thing of all. Now let's get down off this cliff. I'm finding those tombs rather depressing.'

'Sarcophagi,' I said. 'The word means "eaters of flesh". Just like your mother.'

April, 1988

From Delphi we went (*en route* for Olympus) to Volos. Once upon a time, O. told me, when he had been on some NATO exercise in Greece some twenty years before, it had been a charming seaside town. Not any more, we found. The Xenia by the shore was closed and falling to pieces. The little park in front of the museum (closed) was as liberally littered with filth as the public gardens in Trogir. The harbour was full of rusty cargo boats, discharging waste like ulcers discharging pus. A hellish collection of factories congested all approaches, but eventually gave way to suburbs that consisted of flat-roofed houses, out of which protruded spikes and wires and cables all ready for the next festering storey to be slammed on the top.

'Why on earth have we come here?' I said.

'Be patient, old bean. A few miles out of this town there is a deserted road that takes us to Argolasti and round most of a delicious peninsula. It was there I took my company for the manoeuvre which I told you of. You are to be treated to military reminiscence.'

And indeed, once one had driven a few miles east of Volos, the coast road was enchanting, twisting in and out of little bays, tunnelling through the olive groves. After a time it turned up on to the ridge which ran down the centre of the peninsula, then descended on to the north coast. Absolute peace; a total and delectable absence of humanity.

'Of course,' said O., 'the tourist season will start soon. Even twenty years ago they had tourists. Now: you see that notice which points to a caravan park?'

'Yes.'

'In 1968 it was just a camping site, with a small administrative centre which contained three offices together with the loos and showers and so on. The Greek Army commandeered half the site for our tents, and also took over two of the offices for my personal billet and company headquarters, and most of the loos and whatnot. It was late September and the tourists were trickling away, so there was no shortage of space and amenity for anyone...until some communist from Volos started to get up trouble. He waited until the company was away up North for a couple of days, doing some practice parachute jumps on the plain of Trikkala before the real manoeuvre started, and then arrived with two bus loads of "deprived children" from Thessalonika and demanded that they should be accommodated in my company area. The officer commanding the rear guard, a very civil subaltern who actually spoke some Greek, told him that there was plenty of room for his party in the section still reserved for the general public. But where were the tents? said the communist. It was understood, said the rear guard commander, that the public provided their own tents.

' "But I have none. I have these children to shelter. I must have some of *those*."

'The communist pointed to ours.

' "Those," explained the rear guard commander, as civil as ever, "are the property of the British War Department. However," – remembering our instructions to foster good relations with the public – "I have got some smaller tents, for use of troops in action, and I can lend them to you for one week, after which they will be needed by the company for Exercise Argos" (as the big manoeuvre had been named).

'This offer was ungraciously accepted. However, when the main body of the company returned the men had no difficulty in making friends with the "deprived children", many of whom were female and most of whom were surprisingly well grown. And indeed it became evident before very long, from the confidences of the "children" themselves, that they were university students on vacation and were there as part of an amateurish plot to disrupt Exercise Argos. This they told my boys while their leader was absent on some subversive mission in Larissa, making no secret of it as they regarded the whole thing as some kind of picnic got up for their benefit, and thought that their sole disruptive function would be to carry a few banners and make a few protesting noises from time to time. And so they lived alongside my soldiers happily enough, and for two days and two nights there was much merry drinking in local taverns and much jolly bucolic behaviour all over the camp.

'Then two things happened,' said O. 'The leader of the "deprived children" returned from Larissa and was promptly told by informers of the fraternisation that had occurred; and I received orders that I must take my company into the field in thirty-six hours' time, equipped with, among other things, the little "pup tents" which had been lent to the "deprived children"…lent, as you will recall, for one week only. That week now being about to expire and our departure for Exercise Argos being imminent, I went to the communist youth leader, with my subaltern who spoke Greek, and politely requested the return of our property in accordance with the agreement.'

A hundred yards below the road, the sea ambled into a rocky cove. A furlong over to the left was a barbed-wire fence, running down to the cove and also along the road, which guarded the entire boundary of the caravan site.

'In those days,' said O., 'there were no fences or nasties of that kind. Just an area in which people pitched their tents. No guardians: they had cheerfully sloped off and left the running of the camp to us. They would in any case have departed at about this time in September, as few tourists were now expected and those no doubt capable of taking care of themselves. No one had warned me about the two bus loads of "deprived children": no one now appeared to make any pronouncement, official or otherwise, as to their rights and status. But one thing was clear enough: they couldn't be allowed to hang on to seventy-five British Army pup tents which had been lent to them out of sheer kindness.'

'Tricky,' I said to O.

'Not tricky at all.'

'But you said just now you'd been ordered to maintain the best possible relations with the Greek public. A row of this kind was the last thing you wanted.'

'Who said anything about a row? As I say, I went to the leader of the "deprived children", used my Greek-speaking subaltern as interpreter, and through him very politely requested the return of my pup tents – or individual field shelters, as they were named on the stores list – because we were now going to need them to go on to the big manoeuvre. Then the youth leader did what he was bound to do: he had the seventy odd tents on loan to his children collected and returned. They were in passable condition, bar a few cigarette burns and some twisted tackle – nothing that couldn't be set right in a few minutes.'

'So far no trouble then.'

'No. Until my own men, who had of course got very attached to the "children", started forming up at company HQ and saying, Look, sir, we are worried about what is to happen to our little pals now they have no tents. Finally, in order to alleviate concern and to maintain morale, I agreed that the "children" should be allowed to move into the much larger tents which my men slept in while in base encampment on the site: There had been no pressure from the "children" themselves nor from their communist leader: I had been more or less compelled to make this concession by the good nature of my own men, who would not be happy if they went away to the manoeuvre leaving their playmates in distress. So a little while later I took the company off to do mock battle on Exercise Argos and left a holding party on the camp site which, once more, was commanded by my Greek-speaking subaltern. He was assisted, I should tell you, by one serjeant and the usual group of idle but intelligent men who make a profession of being left behind on rear parties. An interesting breed this: they are at once totally reliable and absolutely worthless, shirkers of the shabbiest kind yet highly accurate and competent caretakers. Every army despises them, no army could do without them – as indeed was soon to be made clear in the case in hand.

'When the company and I had been gone two days, a self-important group of publicity liaison officers arrived with a collection of British journalists. They were a pretty decent lot as journalists go (as my subaltern was to tell me later) and definitely on their best behaviour, enjoying their jaunt and eager to sing sweetly for their supper. But there was one joker in the pack – a chap who wasn't really a journalist at all but a military historian who had somehow wangled his ticket. My sensible subaltern read the fellow's number at once, and went out of his way to be more civil and accommodating than ever, while preparing himself for embarrassing questions. For while all the journalists and staff officers accepted and even applauded our act of kindness to the "deprived children", this historian – Vallis, he was called, Horace Vallis – was determined to find fault. Soon enough he got together with the communist youth leader, who told him a damaging tale: many of his "children", claimed the communist, had been enticed by my soldiers, and it was in order to curry favour and persuade him to keep the thing quiet that I, as company commander, had provided tents for his group.

'And in a way, you see, this was hideously plausible. My men had, in a sense, "enticed" the "children": the fact that they weren't really "children" and had cooperated most heartily in their own "enticement" was not an easy point to make in the face of the moral suspicion which Vallis was spreading among the publicity party. Why should he want to make trouble for us? you well may ask: he was there on a magnificent freebie, courtesy of Whitehall, he was not expected to write a report or anything tiresome like that, he was simply being taken round, at considerable expense, to imbibe military *esprit* and so refresh his own creative spirit – and yet he couldn't mind his own business or leave well alone. And since he was an important man in his profession (or else he would not have been there at all) he had to be listened to. The brigadier who was in charge of the party would have to listen, the journalists would have to listen (for although all of them might prefer not to listen, they could not afford the risk of being later accused of moral insouciance). There were the makings of a blazing moral scandal here and the first heretic that would be led to the stake was *me*.

'But this, of course, is just the kind of situation in which the scrimshankers and skivers who make up rear parties are expert in dealing with. They are natural survivors, lovers of a quiet life, inveterate respecters of the *status quo ante*, the sworn enemies of pryers and prodnosers. My subaltern consulted the serjeant: obviously, he said, the communist youth leader had now found the perfect material to disseminate in all directions and the perfect medium, in Vallis, through whom to disseminate it. For any number of reasons Doctor Horace Vallis, Ph.D., author of the prestigious bestsellers, *Flanders Poppies* and *Korean Counterpoint*, must be stopped. How? Leave it to us, sir.

'The publicity party was apparently due to spend a day and a night and the next morning on our peninsula (though there had been no advance warning of its arrival), this because of the great beauty of the situation. "I'll provide a bit of beauty, sir," said the serjeant to my subaltern.

'Now, among the "deprived children", there were some who indeed were still legally children. A suitably decorative twelve-year-old was bribed, briefed and installed under the mosquito net in Vallis' tent while Vallis was still out drinking. The serjeant and several concealed witnesses were on hand when Vallis came blundering into his tent and failed to light the storm lantern which had been deliberately fixed. As he scrabbled his way naked (pyjamas not to be found) under the net, the torches shone out and a camera clicked. Vallis, knowing that he had been framed, yet found it expedient to withdraw his complaint about the conduct of my company; and the publicity party went more or less merrily on its way after an early luncheon the next morning.'

'And what,' I said after a long silence, 'do we deduce from all of that?'

'We deduce, old bean, that you arty types are unpredictable and often malicious: why should Vallis have wanted to make a row about my soldiers' harmless amusements? And we deduce that soldiers, even the least dutiful and energetic of them, are faithful to their unit and their commander.'

'Does the point need making so elaborately?'

'Yes. In the course of this journey you have extolled Catullus, who put his poetry above military and family obligations; and you have approved Timandros, who used his knowledge of poetry to desert his comrades. So now I am providing an instance on the other side. I am saying that a loyal and obedient soldier is to be preferred to a poet or artist, however talented, who proves treacherous.'

'An artist must be treacherous to his fellow men because it is his function to escape from forlorn reality. He makes it up to the human race by offering his escape route for the use of all.'

'You're just being clever. Most human beings are too simple, too much tied to reality by their obligations, to be able to take any escape routes.'

'Too prejudiced, you mean; too blind and clumsy to follow the artist in his flight.'

'Too decent.'

'Too stupid.'

'Too steadfast.'

'Too dull.'

'Right,' said O. 'We shall have a duel about this. Chess. How do we stand?'

'I have won sixteen games, you have won three and one was drawn by perpetual check.'

'Sixteen and a half to three and a half. You are 1,300 guineas ahead.'

'I thought you refused to play for money.'

'A duel,' said O., ignoring my last remark, 'which will be ordered as follows. We shall play chess, when we reach Olympus tomorrow, for double or quits on 1,300 guineas. The soldier – me – versus the artist – you. Trial by combat: to vindicate the shining beacon of the soldiers' honour against the *ignis fatuus* of the artist and the poet.'

March, 1962

As soon as we reached Venice, O. bought his birthday present for his mother.

The journey from Corfu had not been agreeable. Although O. had kept his word and spent every night in the back of the Traveller, he had used my hotel bedroom as a place of hygiene and recuperation, ruthlessly and without payment. His one meal a day had certainly consisted of bread and salami: this did not preclude his scrounging half of mine. Brindisi, Foggia, Pesaro and Rovigo (in those days there was no *autostrada* up the east coast of Italy) are none of them my favourite places; the attendance of O. in his role of crazed and hovering harpy did little to improve them.

And then, Venice. O. decided that a suitable birthday gift for Mummy would be a small bale of fine material from Fortuny: price, 76,500 lire, in 1962 an enormous sum. O. scraped it together: he sent off the bale; followed it with messages of love and longing; and took his last £10 Travellers' Cheque to the casino out on the Lido to turn it into enough to pay his way for the rest of the journey home.

'Lend me a tenner,' he said when he had lost his own.

'If you lose another tenner, we shall have to go to the Consulate and beg for money. That will not look good when it is reported to the War Office.'

'*You* can go to the Consulate. I'll keep out of it.'

'How sensible of you.'

He lost another tenner. In fact we still had just enough to get us home, but I wasn't letting on.

'Chuck over another tenner,' said O. a few minutes later. 'I feel a winning streak coming on. And if we've got to go to the Consul, we may as well have a bit of fun first.'

'You're having the fun and I shall have to go to the Consul.'

'Well,' said O., 'it's all your fault. Making me spend all that money on my bloody old mother. If you hadn't been so aggressive about Apollo and the male principle and women just being senseless wombs, I shouldn't have reacted like that.'

'I was only explaining a bit of primitive theology.'

'You shouldn't be so *teaching*, that's what. And a fellow don't like to be told that his mother is just a dumb, amorphous vagina.'

'If only she was.'

'Here, here. Anyway,' said O. cheerfully, 'I've got her out of my system for a bit. Generosity has cancelled guilt. Not that she'll be grateful, mind you. Shall we really have to go to the Consul for money?'

'No. Not if we leave this casino *now*.'

'One more tenner?'

'NO.'

'Tell you what. You're in a funk about going to the Consul.'

'So would you be. They turn very nasty when you ask for money. They confiscate your passport.'

'Then how do you get into England?'

'They give you a special identity card, valid for just long enough to get you home.'

'What's the matter with that? Here we are in this lovely casino and we can't play any more roulette because you are fussing about your passport.'

'Look,' I said. 'It costs 200 lire to ride back from here to Venice on the *vaporetto*. If you don't come now, I shall leave you here...and you haven't even got 200 lire to pay your fare across the Lagoon.'

'200 lire is nothing.'

'You still haven't got it.'

'You'd desert me? On my mother's birthday? We were going to have a special dinner – remember?'

'I thought you'd got over all that nonsense about your mother.'

'I was still looking forward to our dinner. I'm afraid you'll have to pay...only until we get back to England, of course. I'm told they do you rather well for grub in Harry's Bar. Green taglialini...fresh lobsters...genuine scampi, not just ageing prawns.'

'We shall be lucky if we can afford a soup kitchen.'

In the end we blew what was left at Harry's and I had to go to the Consul. I was interviewed by the Vice-Consul, whom I'd known and hated at Cambridge.

'You always were a pretty sloppy sort of chap,' he said. 'And a cadger. I remember your hanging about by the porters' lodge begging for half-crowns to pay for your lunch.'

'I shall only need twenty quid.'

'Twenty quid. You still haven't paid my half-crown back.'

'I don't owe you one. You were about the only chap in the college who never contributed.'

'This chap you're with? The one who owns the car?'

'In the army,' I said treacherously.

'Officer?'

'Since when did Other Ranks have cars?' (They didn't then, which made life a great deal pleasanter.)

'I'll pay out twenty quid from the Special Repatriation Fund. I don't give a damn about you, but we can't have the Queen's officers hanging about like hoboes in Venice. He must surrender his officers' identity card. We'll send it on when he pays back the FO.'

'He won't like that. He'll get an adverse report.'

Yet after all, I thought, he had richly deserved it. Or had he? Perhaps I shouldn't have talked so disrespectfully of mothers. But my remarks had been purely academic, to start with, contrasting the functions of Apollo with those of Rhea or Gē, the earth-mother. How was I to know that such an innocent exercise would lead to all this pother? The only way not to initiate disaster, I thought, as I went outside to fetch O. and his identity card, was never to open one's mouth at all except to put food in it. All speech was made at the risk of evil and misfortune: in the Beginning was the Word.

April, 1988

Olympus at last. Where were the gods whom I had come, on behalf of the *Daily Telegraph*, to investigate? They were sulking behind a layer of cloud, which began at Litokhoron (1,000 feet up) and continued to the summit. Any investigation of the gods must wait until the cloud cleared, which might take anything up to a month. Meanwhile, there was the trial by combat with O., the battle over the chessboard in which he stood for the army and I stood for artists, a battle which would be worth 1,300 guineas, double or quits on O.'s existing debt. Having installed ourselves in the best of the dismal hotels in Litokhoron (a decaying health resort) we sat down by a window with a magnificent view of thick yellow fog. Are you there, almighty Zeus? O Hermes, Athena, Apollo, are you all there? Those that ask silly questions, I thought, sometimes get very surprising answers. So I invoked the aid of the gods for my contest and turned with some relief from the billowing bile outside to look over the sixteen charming pieces – O.'s white, mine black, as the draw had decided.

O. commenced with one of his vigorous queen and bishop onslaughts. Having just remembered in time how to frustrate both fool's mate and scholar's mate, I settled down to construct a solid pawn formation on the queen's side. O. castled on the king's side, to bring a rook into play and exert additional pressure. All he needed now to achieve a very strong position was to bring his queen's bishop out to balance the king's. But before he could do this, he must advance his queen's knight's pawn, either to QKt 3, in which case I could take it with my pawn on QR 5, or to QKt 4, in which case I could take it *en passant*, in either case establishing my pawn on QKt 6, where it would be very threatening indeed. Quite apart from anything else, my queen's rook would now dominate its file.

In the event, O. advanced his queen's knight's pawn to QKt 4; I took it as planned, *en passant* with my pawn from QR 5.

'What sort of a move is that?' said O.

'I have taken your pawn *en passant*.'

'Never heard of it.'

'If a pawn is moved forward two squares, from its initial position, and the first of these is diagonally threatened by your opponent's pawn, yours can be taken *en passant*.'

'Who says?'

'The book of laws of chess says.'

'You're certain?'

'Certain.'

'You haven't got a book of the laws here?'

'I don't carry one around.'

'You realise that this move of yours – this taking *en passant* of which I have never heard in all my life – '

' – A lot of people haven't – '

' – Absolutely buggers me up. I am virtually certain to lose my queen's rook. You are virtually certain to get a pawn promoted to queen. And all because I didn't know you could take my pawn…*en passant*.'

This is true, I thought. It's only a matter of luck that it hasn't come up before – if only it had. He didn't just miscalculate when he made that disastrous move. He's too good a natural player for that. He really did not know that in certain circumstances a pawn can take a pawn *en passant*. I must offer to call the game void. Come to that, if he's been playing in such ignorance (albeit it has affected no other game) I should offer him his entire losses back. I can't take 2,600 guineas off a person who is genuinely ignorant of one section of the laws of chess.

I opened my mouth to make the offer – and closed it again.

It's his fault, I thought. I told him a simple tale about how a prisoner in Sicily was released as a reward for spouting Euripides and he gets into a huff because other prisoners weren't so lucky. He says the military code requires this, that and the other, tells tall stories about his company in Volos, gets into a bate when I am not much impressed and challenges me to this 'duel', plain and honourable soldier versus clever and fraudulent artist. He made this challenge. So be it.

O. was rummaging in his suitcase.

'I suppose,' he was saying, 'that a lot of people would require to be shown the book of laws in a case as unusual as this, but I've known you too long to bother about that. We were, after all, in the same regiment even if you were scarcely a creditable member of it. Ah, here we are.'

He produced a cheque book. He wrote out a cheque for Two Thousand, Seven Hundred and Thirty Pounds – 2,600 guineas.

'I recognise,' he said, 'that the position is hopeless. Here is your cheque. If you post it from Greece at express rates,' he said, 'it will be in your bank in just a few days. Don't try to register it. If you register a letter in Greece, they require to know what is inside it. Once they find a cheque, they will accuse you of illegally sending money out of Greece.'

'What rubbish,' I said, rather stupefied by the whole proceeding. 'It's a cheque drawn on your bank in England directing payment of funds into mine. It has nothing to do with the Greeks at all.'

'Nevertheless, that is how they will regard the matter. I found that out in 1968, when trying to send funds from here to the mother of one of my soldiers, who was in trouble over some girl. Greeks are imbeciles in this matter — indeed in most, if not in all. So express this, but do not ask to register it.'

'If it were stolen…?'

'It would be refused by my bank. I have made it very clear that it is to be paid into your account only. Just in case, I shall send a letter to the bank myself, repeating the instruction on the face of the cheque.'

'I… I…'

'Don't bother to say anything. You have won this fair and square, and there's an end of that.'

Although the artist has won the duel, I thought, the soldier carries off the palm of honour. But then the soldier always does. Artists and intellectuals jeer: the soldier faces the bullets in their defence. Such a simple, obvious point. Why do so few artists and intellectuals admit it? Sheer irritation, I thought, because the soldier is so damned smug.

PART FOUR

Isherwood Gored

'If you like,' said the studio representative, 'we can send a girl over to the Beverly Hills Hotel to help you with the typing.'

'I think I can manage it myself.'

'You're sure now?'

'Oh yes.'

'Well, that's up to you. We thought you might like company. With a little persuasion and a drink or two, she'd probably go down on you.'

'It's very kind of you,' I said, 'but I think I'd better stick to the job myself.'

The studio representative laughed stridently down the telephone.

'Suit yourself, Si,' he said.

For the first time in my life I was in Hollywood, or thereabouts, trying to write a film script, or at any rate a treatment for one. The book that was to be filmed was Gore Vidal's *Burr*. I now rang up old chum, Howard.

'Gore there?' I asked.

'Yes. He's having his portrait done. Or rather, a preliminary drawing. By Chris Isherwood's friend, Don. And Mistress Tynan is here too.'

'What does she want?'

'What does anyone want?' said Howard. 'Fame and fortune.'

'So since Gore's clearly a bit preoccupied, perhaps you can answer a question for me. The studio representative has offered to send me a girl to help with my typing. He says that "she might go down on me". What does that mean?'

'*Soixante-neuf* without the *neuf*. When is she coming?'

'She isn't. I declined.'

'Very prudent, I'd say,' said Howard, who enjoyed an Anglicism from time to time. 'Those girls are not for you.'

'Unhygienic?'

'Not physically. Mentally. Once they start they won't stop. They want to prove something.'

'What?'

'Difficult. Let's put it this way. I have a friend who comes around from time to time. He is taking a course in muscle building. He has an excellent degree from Yale, no less, in mathematics and physics, but all he can think about is muscle building. He wants to be a professional wrestler or a weight lifter. Yale has offered him an important teaching post with plenty of time for research. All he thinks about is staying here in California and lifting weights. When I ask him why, he says, "Because I'm sick". Asked to elucidate, he says that he wants to prove that he can do it. He knows he can do math and physics, you see, so there is no point in going on with them. He doesn't know yet whether he can become a pro wrestler and he wants to find out.'

'Why wrestling?' I said. 'Or weight lifting, come to that?'

'Because he was a skinny, weedy boy and everyone at Groton laughed at his drumstick arms and legs. So he has this obsession, to prove that he too can be like Joe Louis. Same with those girls from the studio pool. They were brought up real nice, most of them. So now they have to convince themselves that they can go down on a guy all day long. It means they're liberated – they think. Like those queens that go running and skipping into the naughty part of the park six times a day. *They* have to convince themselves not only that they're liberated but that they're still capable of doing it. Reassurance, that's what all these people want. And of course the more they get reassured the less convincing the reassurance. Mistress T. with her writing, or those studio girls with their gobbling, or my friend with his muscles, or those queens with their antics – they're all watching pots that take longer and longer to boil each time and finally will go dry before they do boil. It's called the law of diminishing returns. The only thing that doesn't diminish is the degree of mental sickness. What are *you* queer for? What's your obsession?'

'Peace and quiet,' I said.

'A people hater, eh? People hater, reader of books, onanist, gambler, lone drinker. Right?'

'Not far out,' I said.

'Solitary cathedral and museum crawler?'

'Yes. I thought I'd go to the Getty Memorial Museum. Since no one's coming here to go down on me, I shall have plenty of time to do my work *and* take the afternoon off.'

'The Getty Memorial Museum?' said Howard. 'All on your own? Boy oh boy oh boy, are you sick?'

In the gas-guzzling monster I had hired from Hertz, it was impossible to turn the wireless off without turning off the whole engine. You could change stations but you couldn't have silence. If you turned the knob to where there wasn't a station – which was a labour of Hercules – you got a mournful bleeping noise that was even worse. So all the way along Sunset Boulevard to the Pacific Ocean I had compulsory music and chitchat, which were, however, interrupted every seven minutes or so by a far superior entertainment in the form of the local news. From this it appeared that an aphrodisiac artist was infesting the campuses of California, doping and having his wicked will with the more succulent students of either sex, leaving them bound and gagged, naked and, when male, priapic (from the residue of the julep), in witty places like the Principal's comfort station. What lifted him to a very high level of comedy, indeed of wizardry, was the incredible ubiquity of the fellow. In the first item I heard about him he had apparently just finished doing his number in a campus cafeteria near Los Angeles; seven minutes later it was announced that fresh and typical victims had just been discovered way up the West Coast. During my (admittedly lethargic) run between Beverly Hills

Hotel and the sea, he had scored some nine or ten times, an average, say, of 1.29 victims every seven minutes, in venues which varied from Berkeley to San Clementis.

Pondering on this versatile exhibition, I turned into the entrance of the Getty Memorial Museum and was stopped at a barrier by a courteous but very firm black man. Had I, he enquired, fixed my reservation? No, I hadn't. Well, he explained, what I should have done was to request the bell captain of my hotel to ring up the museum and arrange a parking reservation. Normally, my gas guzzler and I would not be admitted without one. However, since I was a guest in the country and since today there were plenty of spaces free, he himself would now allot me one. No, there was no charge.

I parked my vehicle on the numbered rectangle I had been appointed to (feeling like a captain who has finally docked an aircraft carrier) and wandered through an open court with many pools and fountains. I couldn't see whether it was intended to be late Roman or early Renaissance (the former, I fancy); either way I found it very agreeable. Acquaintances had told me it was vulgar, but when, I ask you, did a little vulgarity do any harm? At the bottom of the court and at the entrance of the museum proper, I was asked for my reservation number and waved on my way, still free of charge.

It had now been made clear to me, by the black man and a number of notices, that only those who arrived in cars or taxis were admitted to the museum at all. In certain cases, a certificate of travel by public transport (what there was of it) would be allowed as *bona fides* for admission; in no case whatever would a pedestrian be let in. It soon became clear to me why not. Whatever one might have thought of the exhibits (and, candidly, in 1979 they were mostly rather draggy sticks of furniture, as Howard might have said), there was no question about the sumptuous amenity. Restaurants, rest rooms, halls of repose…all invited the jaded sightseer to relaxation and indulgence with the dreamy magic of Spenser's Garden of

Adonis or Bower of Bliss. The wonder was that anyone did any sightseeing at all. Now, clearly the place would have been a paradise for travel-worn hippies or whomever, a danger fully realised and guarded against by the administration on behalf of Mr Getty. No pedestrians here; I should just think not.

Reflecting on the uses of democracy, I relieved myself among imperial pillars, ate an elaborate snack under titanic murals and then sat down to recuperate from these adventures in a *trompe-l'oeil* grove of tamarisk, where I might admire primly tripping nymphs and satyrs, and listen to a somewhat repetitious recorded nightingale.

Back in my aircraft carrier and reluctantly leaving the many-sounding seashore for the depths of LA, I was once more diverted by the antics of the Campus Comus, who had had several further triumphs while I was lolling in the Getty Museum. The trouble was, he was now losing his good taste and sense of humour. He was choosing elderly, ugly and sickly victims, and abandoning them in nasty situations, such as the municipal rubbish dump. Since incidents were now spread over hundreds of square miles, it had at last been deduced that there was either a copy-cat sequence in progress or else that there was a syndicate of widely separated members. That a rogue rapist was now committing vicious acts of cruelty was giving concern and spoiling the joke; and of course before I even got back to Beverly Hills, someone had overdone it and actually throttled a lady in her nineties, then chopped her up and been apprehended feeding her minced fesses to the tigers in his local zoo. A sad end, I thought, to a very passable jape: why are Americans always so excessive?

Soon after I was back in my room, Howard rang up. Apparently Gore had excited Don (Isherwood's portrait-making friend) with the news that I had known E. M. Forster at King's College, Cambridge. Don had departed bubbling with the intention of imparting this news to Christopher, who had 'adored' Morgan Forster.

'But Isherwood knew this perfectly well already,' I told Howard. 'One of the very few times I ever met him was with Morgan Forster…who was giving us a dinner of spectacular sparseness in his rooms in King's.'

'I thought your college did that sort of thing rather well,' said Howard, who knew the proper form.

'It does. Morgan Forster didn't. He was the meanest man that ever drew breath.'

'Ah. That is Gore's view. He has decided to ask you and Christopher and Don to a little dinner to discuss the matter – and indeed assess Forster from several other aspects.'

'Aren't you coming?'

'No. I'm spending the evening with my muscle man. How are you getting on with *Burr*?'

'All right. The structure of the novel is rather complex.'

'The studio will like that. They think complexity of structure is a sign of important literature.'

'But do they want it in a script?'

'They will tell you they do. In fact what they want is something very simple and easy to follow but which keeps changing direction.'

'*Burr* is a story within a story. What shall I do about that?'

'Cut from one to the other,' said Howard, with the assurance of Gore himself.

'That means flashbacks,' I said wearily. 'Everyone hates flashbacks these days.'

'You sound a bit low. I told you that going to the Getty Museum would do you no good.'

'I had an interesting time in the car,' I said defensively, 'listening to radio reports about that man who's cruising around with the aphrodisiac.'

'There are dozens of them. There must be,' said Howard.

'They've caught one of them.'

'That won't stop the rest. It's become a craze. Before you can say "Morgan Forster" everyone will be joining in. Californians are very imitative. The trouble is that it will create such a bad impression, coming at the time of Princess Margaret Rose's visit.'

'We don't call her that any more. Just Princess Margaret.'

'What a pity. The rose is the emblem of England.'

'Perhaps she doesn't want to be the emblem of England any more,' I said, 'now that it's so disgusting.'

'My word, you are low. Let's hope this dinner party will cheer you up.'

'Why should talking about E. M. Forster cheer anybody up?'

'You can talk about Princess Margaret Rose as well. Gore knows her, you know. He may be going to give a party for her. Do you know her?'

'No. But I was once quite near to her in King's chapel. She was with her parents in the Provost's box, and I was just below in a scholar's stall. I'll never forget it. I got so nervous that I had to go out to pee in the middle of the "Nunc Dimittis".'

'Was there comment on the platform?'

'No. Since I was a scholar I was a steward for the royal occasion. I just walked out with a purposeful look as if I was on steward's business, like ejecting someone that was being sick. If you act strictly in your official character no one ever notices you.'

'So Princess Margaret Rose didn't notice you?'

'Nor did the King; nor did the Queen; nor did the Provost, or I should have been told off afterwards.'

'But how do you know the Royals' – well done, Howard – 'didn't see you? They would have been much too polite to tell you off afterwards. Did Morgan Forster come to the service?'

'No.'

'How rude.'

'He didn't approve of the Chapel and he didn't approve of Royalty.'

'Did he approve of you?'

'No. I tried to borrow money from him.'

'If he was as mean as you say, you must have known it wouldn't be any good.'

'I was desperate. I went round the college calling on everyone I knew. He was on staircase A, so he was the first. A very discouraging start: he said that he wasn't interested in me or my money.'

'Well, well, well,' said Howard. 'You'll have a lot to tell Christopher. Would you like to come to Gore's party for Princess Margaret Rose? You could ask whether she noticed when you walked out during the "Nunc Dimittis".'

'That was in 1951. She might not remember.'

'Well, think about it. The party, I mean. Meanwhile, this dinner for discussion of Forster is the day after tomorrow. Gore is taking you all to a Mexican restaurant where they have Tequila.'

'What's that?'

'A Mexican spirit. Malcolm Lowry, the *Underneath the Volcano* man, used to get sozzled on it. This restaurant you're going to uses it in long drinks. They taste delicious but they're lethal.'

'Thank you for the tip.'

'One more thing,' Howard said. 'Gore will pick you up in a taxi at eight o'clock and will brief you about Christopher on the way. The thing is, you see, that Christopher is very sensitive about being English. He can't forgive or forget all those nasty things which English people like Evelyn Waugh said about him and Auden at the beginning of the war.'

'What else did he expect?'

'You must try not to make any mention of it in front of Christopher. I'll leave Gore to explain the details.'

'The point is,' Gore told me as we drove to the Mexican restaurant in our taxi, 'that to Christopher and all that lot their decision to break with England and settle over here was the crisis of their lives. Never mind that it was forty years ago, that everyone else in the US and the UK has long forgotten the whole business, *they* think that the world is still discussing it as assiduously and as ferociously as in 1939. Therefore they are perpetually on edge, ever ready to take umbrage and make aggressive scenes. Somebody was talking about Aldous Huxley the other day, saying that it was possible to take two views of his mescalin caper: the first, that it was a valuable and courageous exploration of the frontier territories of the mind; and the second, that it was all a farrago of nonsense and set a very bad example to the young, who now swim in all kinds of dope on the specious excuse of spiritual experiment. Christopher, who was present, flew into a temper and said that this second opinion was simply a rehash of the British prejudice against Huxley: they'd never forgiven him for getting out of England just before the war, Christopher said, and they'd always belittled and ridiculed his splendid research with mescalin out of sheer spite. Then the chap who had made the original comment on Huxley said that he wasn't thinking about any of that, he was simply making a common-sense assessment of a kind which, sixteen years after Huxley's death, was very much called for. Whereupon Christopher muttered and gibbered and eventually went off in a sulk. In one word, he is still paranoid.'

'Tonight,' I said, 'we are to discuss E. M. Forster. I don't think any of that war-time bit need come into it at all.'

'But, dear boy, that's the whole point about Christopher. Everything, from Greek tragedy to the Quantum theory, is sooner or later reduced by him into terms of his own epic struggle – as he sees it – to break free from England, the land of the copybook headings, and escape to America, land of the equal and the free. Now, you've only met him once or twice, I gather, and not for very long: so you'll find he will not rest, or let you rest, until he can extract an opinion from you about that seminal period of his life and his migration to the US.'

'I take the Evelyn Waugh line,' I said, 'and have done ever since I read *Put Out More Flags* at the age of seventeen, when the war was just ending. Auden and Isherwood equal Parsnip and Pimpernel.'

'I.e., Auden and Isherwood were just a couple of fags who chickened out?'

'Right.'

'You'll oblige me by keeping this sentiment to yourself during this dinner. He is, after all, my guest.'

'That I appreciate and of course I shall suppress discourteous utterance in the matter. But what act do you want me to put on instead?'

'Just pretend you were too young to know about it.'

'If he thinks all this is as important as you say he does, he'll be pretty offended by that.'

'You can imply,' said Gore, 'that the whole thing is simply accepted by your contemporaries as a *fait accompli.*'

'If I've got you right, he wants to be applauded, not just accepted.'

'What view did Forster take?'

'Difficult to say. Any talk of the war made him feel inferior. He loathed any reminder that a lot of us had been officers during or just after it. He took the Chinese view, I think, that all soldiers were quite ridiculous. There's a lot to be said for it, as you'll know for yourself having been one. But when there is a war, soldiers are necessary – a simple fact that Forster couldn't really bear to admit. I'd say that his view was that now the war was over we must just pretend it never happened. You see, not only did mention of the war make him feel inferior, it made him jealous, just as Cyril Connolly was jealous of an old friend's armoured car. It was something that took people's minds off *him.*'

'So as far as all that goes, he would probably have approved of Christopher's desertion?'

'Yes. But I can't think that any of this will be very fruitful ground. What needs to be discussed is Morgan Forster's capacity for being a silly, interfering old woman…and his admiration of "Goldie" Lowes-Dickinson, who was an absolute embarrassment to anyone who was any kind of a man at all – homosexual or other. There was a large section of the world they just didn't know about or acknowledge – the world of action. Not only soldiers upset them, but barristers, huntsmen, explorers, scientists, politicians, sportsmen – anyone that actually *did* anything. All Forster and Co were ever good for was to sit about having lovely thoughts, and to complain about those that moved about a bit on the ground that they made a noise, and then Forster and Lowes-Dickinson couldn't hear each other twittering.'

'Well, just play it by ear, dear boy. But remember that Christopher adored Morgan Forster and he's an old man who mustn't be unduly upset.'

'Goodnight, Mr Vidal,' said the taxi driver as we got out at Montezuma's Human Abattoir.

Gore liked to be recognised: a good start, I thought, to the evening.

In the end, the discussion about Morgan Forster took a line that no one could have predicted or even deemed possible. It was, as it happened, my fault.

Asked by Isherwood how well I had known Morgan at King's, and seeking about for a pleasant and not wholly boring answer, I remarked that we had once been to the cinema together, on my suggestion, and that Morgan had seemed to enjoy the film.

'And what film was that?' said Christopher.

'Walt Disney's *Peter Pan*,' I said.

In fact this was untrue. The film we had been to was Alfred Hitchcock's *Strangers on a Train*, a marvellous thriller which Morgan, despite his dislike of violence, had indeed appeared to enjoy, possibly because of its artistry. *Peter Pan* I had seen with Morgan's old chum, J. R. (Joe) Ackerley. Since I closely associated the two men in my memory, I had mixed up which film I went to with which and now saw no particular reason to correct my error – indeed, as it turned out, had no time to.

'Morgan,' said Isherwood, 'would never have gone to any rubbish of Barrie's.'

'I suggested it,' I replied. 'He had never seen a full-length animated cartoon before and I thought it might amuse him.'

'How could it have done? Just before the war I once proposed that we should go to *Snow White and the Seven Dwarves*, which was the first full-length cartoon ever to be made. He replied that he didn't like those Germanic sort of fairy tales in which the heroine is turned into a corpse – even if the prince does revive her later.'

'But that was an objection to those grisly stories by Anderson or Grimm,' said Gore, 'not to the idea of a full-length cartoon. After all, he might have liked the idea of *Peter Pan* done in such an unfamiliar medium.'

'I just told you: he hated J. M. Barrie.'

'So much the more fool him,' said Gore. 'For though I agree that a lot of Barrie is muck, the character of Captain Hook, the old Etonian pirate, is a splendid invention, as is his enemy, the ticking crocodile.'

'Morgan did not like fantasy.'

'But he did. Look at his own. Thomas Browne as the coachman in *The Celestial Omnibus*. All those little boys in Italy that kept on turning into Pan in the middle of picnics and making their aunties hysterical. What is all that if it isn't fantasy?'

'Admirers of E. M. Forster,' said Don carefully, 'are quietly and reluctantly agreed that his stories of that nature are – well – untypical. It is thought that he himself was later embarrassed by them.'

'There are enough of them,' said Gore. 'He made no attempt to have them suppressed. I remember, very clearly, one such story in which the boy who turned into a faun or a satyr or whatever it was put down his Bovril sandwich, stripped naked, and went rushing off to join all the other fauns and satyrs. Somewhere near Florence, that happened.'

'Could you get Bovril in Florence?' enquired Don.

'I was speaking figuratively,' said Gore. 'For "Bovril sandwich" understand appropriate food for a little English boy. Now, anyone who can get up a tale like that about an English prep school boy in Florence for the hols, must surely be able to tolerate *Peter Pan*.'

'You haven't understood me,' said Christopher. 'It is a question of quality. Morgan's fantasy at least had a basis of truth – the existence of the wild creature that lurks in every one of us. *Peter Pan* was just commercial slop.'

'What he seemed to enjoy,' I improvised, 'was that dog, Nana, that took care of the children.'

Montezuma's Human Abattoir was very hot. Gore had just ordered a third round of long Tequila fruit drinks.

'But Morgan hated dogs,' said Christopher, and took a slurp of Tequila plus Tamarind. 'I remember Joe Ackerley saying that he never would have Joe's dog, Queenie, to stay with him. It made for a lot of bad feeling.'

'The thing about that,' I said, 'was that dogs weren't allowed in King's College guest rooms.'

'The other thing was,' said Gore, 'or so I was told by you yourself, that Queenie was almost permanently on heat, and couldn't travel. Joe had to stay in London with her and couldn't go to Cambridge or anywhere else.'

'But that's just it,' said Christopher. 'Morgan bitterly resented the fact that Joe couldn't come to stay because Queenie was on heat. It made him hate Queenie and by extension all other dogs even more than he'd hated them before. He simply cannot have enjoyed the character of Nana.'

115

'What he enjoyed,' I said, 'was the idea of Nana's taking care of the children. He said it reminded him of Romulus and Remus being suckled by a she-wolf, and also of Chiron the Centaur's bringing up Jason and Achilles.'

'I can't relate all this to the Morgan Forster whom I knew,' said Christopher. What with confusion and Tequila, his neck had gone scarlet under his exaggerated crew cut, which was like a pudding-basin job on an aging band-boy.

'I think that what we have to recognise,' said Gore, 'is that Forster was in many ways a very silly man.'

'Inconsistent,' I said, and decided to tell the truth for a while. 'During my last year at Cambridge, there was rather a good comedy on at the Arts Theatre, with Roland Culver, about a member of Parliament who had trouble keeping his wife away from his mistresses, because they all liked each other much better than they liked him, and were forever meeting for giggly lunches and even entire weekends. A pretty flimsy affair but quite witty. When Morgan was asked what he thought of it, he said that he didn't care for the thing because it was full of "immorality flats". He didn't object that the play was frivolous or light-minded or eminently forgettable: simply that it was full of immorality flats, the idea of which he detested. Now, as his friend, Patrick Wilkinson, the Horatian scholar, pointed out very succinctly, Morgan Forster had spent his life in immorality flats. As soon as he got free from his mother, he had immorality flats all over Europe and most noticeably in Alexandria during the First War. He was full of praise for Cavafy and his friends, all of whom lived in immorality flats, and someone in one of his novels – someone he rather likes – keeps a mistress in one. So what on earth was he talking about when he said he detested the idea of them?'

'Precisely,' said Gore. 'He was a man of double standards – one for himself and one for the rest of us. And so intolerant. The only man in his *oeuvre* that ever played a game – the only man in all his books who was a proper man – was killed off almost immediately, "broken up" in a game of rugby football. He had to be punished, you see, for actually doing something, instead of sitting on his arse and bitching about the moral insensitivity of everyone else in a "world of telegrams and anger".'

'You are deliberately distorting it all,' said Christopher as his fourth Tequila (refused by Don and myself) was placed in front of him.'

'I have asked you here purely in order,' said Gore, 'that we may have a quiet and rational talk about Forster.'

'So Don said, and that's why I've come. But all this talk of *Peter Pan* has misled us – it has taken us off down a totally wrong path.'

'Not at all,' said Gore. 'It has compelled us to discuss a side of Morgan Forster that his admirers studiously ignore. A captious and foolish side, puerile, vacuous and winsome; a side that explains the total fiasco of the Malabar Caves, for example, and that quintuply blush-making father and son relationship in *A Room with a View.*'

Christopher took a violent pull at his Tequila, opened his mouth to retort, started wagging his cropped head from side to side like a mechanical clown and toppled into the arms of the expectant Don…who took him out, rather officiously assisted by Gore. I wondered what would have happened if I'd got the thing right at the start and told them all that it was really *Strangers on a Train* which Morgan and I had seen together. As far as I remember, he had much enjoyed the villain's simpering and incestuous mother, so where that would have got us, God knew. Together with the Tequila, I thought, it would probably have got Christopher on the floor, just as *Peter Pan* had.

Gore came back.

'Don's taking him home,' he said. 'A very neat evasion, I thought, of all the problems we discussed on the way here. Did you *really* go to the cinema with Forster?'

'Oh yes.'

And I swear I did. The old Royal in Cambridge.

'Well now. Our next enjoyment. As I think Howard has told you, I shall be giving a party for Princess Margaret. Today week. I'd like you to come.'

'I wrote the script of a serial,' I told him, 'about Edward VIII and Mrs Simpson. The Royal Family didn't enjoy it much, I'm told. Of course, they probably don't know the name of the scriptwriter – nobody ever does – but they just might and then it would be embarrassing for me to meet Princess Margaret.'

'I shall tell her you wrote that script,' Gore said. 'That's why I want you to come – to see what she says to you.'

'I'd much sooner not. I hate parties.'

'You were quite a star at the party we've just had.'

'A small dinner party with people I know is one thing,' I said. 'A crush of celebrities and princesses is quite another. My brother and I used to hide in the lavatory when we went to smart children's parties until it was time to go home. We couldn't even endure the conjuring show – in case the conjuror called one of us out for some trick.'

'You must have grown out of that by now. Someone said you were a great partygoer at Cambridge.'

'For a brief period in my frothy youth. It is long since gone.'

'You can't refuse the Royal Command.'

'It's only your command.'

'Most people in Hollywood would give their eyes to come. Don't you like your Royal Family?'

'I start crying whenever they appear on television. Particularly the Queen Mother.'

'Well then?' said Gore.

'Loyalty is one thing. Introduction is another. Princess Margaret would not want me crying all over her.'

'You won't when it comes to the point.'

'Gore…why are you being so persistent about this?'

'Simon…why are you being so stubborn about this?'

'I told you. I prefer to adore from a distance. Anyway, she hasn't come here to meet Englishmen, but to mix with your lot.'

'The trouble with you is that you're an inverted snob.' Suddenly I had an inspiration. I took out my wallet and showed Gore my air ticket home.

'It's for the day before your party,' I said.

'Change it.'

Christ.

'I'll ring up the airport,' I said feebly.

'No. You'll take your ticket to your bell captain. He'll do it all for you. I'll come in with you when we get to your hotel and give him full instructions.'

The story ends with a whimper. The planes that week were all full. I had to leave on the flight on which my seat had been booked. Why Gore was so keen that I should meet HRH, I shall never know.

He reported to me later on the transatlantic telephone that she had formed a poor impression of *Edward and Mrs Simpson*, complaining that her family did not talk remotely as I had scripted them.

'Ah,' I was able to tell him, 'the director and the actors changed a lot of it. That makes it their fault.'

' "Actors are cattle," as Hitchcock used to say. What a pity they won't believe it.'

'Talking of Hitchcock, I said, 'I can now confess. The film I saw with Morgan Forster was not *Peter Pan* but *Strangers on a Train*.'

'Never mind. Christopher had so much Tequila that he's forgotten the entire story. Don has persuaded him that he argued us into the ground and then fainted because of the heat. There's no truth anywhere these days.'

'None,' I agreed.

'But here's some for free. The chap who was interested in *Burr* has left the studio, having been poached for more cash by another. So they'll never make *Burr* now. The new man won't want his predecessor's leavings. No true Yankee will walk in a dead man's shoes, however well cut.'

'No hope, Gore?'

'No hope, Simon. You won't get half the money you might have done. Neither shall I.'

So if there is little truth in the world there is some justice, I thought, seeing Christopher's crew-cut head as it wagged in despair while he toppled, deceived and helpless, into the arms of his friend.

PART FIVE

He Knew He Was Right

'Colonel Smith, Sir?' said the Serjeant-Major (a very senior man in his grade). 'Colonel Smith?' he said, and thought carefully for a while. 'A gentleman, unlike some we needn't mention at that level or near it. Slow. Steady. Not over bright. Easy in many ways but impatient of contradiction. Why they chose him instead of Major Max, God alone knows.'

'Quite simple. The present CO detests Major Max because Major Max is charming, handsome and popular, and has a brilliant record. DSO and Bar. Commanded a brigade during the war – commanded a division, very briefly, while the GOC was ill. But since Colonel Smith is senior to Major Max, if only by a few days, and since for some reason he holds a Brevet Lieutenant-Colonelcy, the present CO has the chance to put Max down. And he has taken it. The rules say that the senior available officer, of field rank and under that of full colonel, must be chosen to command the battalion unless there is a very good reason why not.'

'Major Max is a very good reason why not. Lieutenant-Colonel Smith is possibly another.'

Warrant officers in our regiment were free with their opinions if they knew one.

'As bad as that?'

'There are many good things about him as I say, sir. But every now and then not always, but every now and then he is determined to have his own way. He becomes…obsessed.'

The takeover happened at Lichfield, in the barracks of one of the Staffordshire regiments, where we were waiting to take ship for Kenya. Our former CO had long since taken his *congé*.

Lieutenant-Colonel Smith arrived unannounced and without fuss in the empty barracks one Sunday afternoon, thus sparing us the trouble of mounting special guards and putting on tedious ceremonies. A good start, it was felt. Smith would live in the officers' mess until we embarked at Liverpool for Mombasa. His own house in Shropshire, where he would leave his family during our tour of duty in Kenya, was too far from Lichfield for convenience – no bad thing, from our point of view, as we should now have an excellent and immediate chance to observe the man, his habits and his foibles.

The man was ordinary enough. His habits and manners were orderly and acceptable. His only foibles (as it appeared in those early days) were quite common in a married infantry officer of little or no private means: firstly, a pretence that not only himself but all other members of the mess lived on the border of extreme poverty and ought to be ashamed of themselves if they didn't; and secondly, a tendency to disapprove of officers who preferred to remain single rather than equip themselves with dowdy and pleasure-inhibiting wives. Smith had a tiresome way of enquiring how soon one was thinking of joining 'the married fraternity'. I myself at that time belonged, in theory, to the 'married fraternity' already; and although Smith was deeply suspicious, because he very soon learned that my wife had not once been seen during the two years odd I had been with the regiment, he could hardly question me as to whether and when I proposed to get myself one. My friend O., when approached in the matter, earned low marks by quoting Shakespeare to the effect that 'a soldier is better accommodated than with a wife'; and a well-known point-to-point rider in the battalion was imprudent enough to observe that he was already married to his favourite mare, and in any case could not afford fodder and stabling for another on two legs.

People forgave Smith for his enquiries on the topic because in most other ways he was undemanding, because he was probably acting on the instructions of the Colonel of the regiment (a well-known hater of bachelors) and because, in any case, since there was nothing whatever either Smith or his superior could do about the matter, his interference was otiose. What we did not forgive Smith quite so easily was his habit of raising his eyebrows whenever anybody ordered a bottle of wine and pointedly calling for beer for himself. This, of course, was part of the poverty act, in which we were all meant to share; but as O. observed, if no one had ordered wine the CO would have had nothing to raise his eyebrows about, so we were probably doing him a good turn. Very likely, said the point-to-point rider, but he wasn't doing us one, looking at our wine like a warlock who wished he knew the spell to turn it sour. Never mind, said O.: so long as he never *did* turn it sour… For myself, I said, I didn't like to feel that I was being grudged any of my enjoyments and there could be no doubt that Smith grudged us this one. However, since in all other things, both on and off parade, he behaved with civil good sense and apparently had no quirks of zealotry, he was rated as harmless enough. Of course, said O., he had rather a lean look; a cosy, pear-shaped colonel would have been more reassuring. Not to worry, said our amateur jockey; Smith's was the rather flabby leanness of the sparse-living desk officer (as he had been for some years), not the black and savage gauntness of the martinet; we could depend on two years' peace and quiet during Smith's incumbency; being asked occasional silly questions about a fellow's (non-existent) marital intentions was a low price to pay.

It was 'Benghazi' Malcolm, our Adjutant, who first alerted me to unsuspected dangers. We were visiting Hereford Cathedral together in order to plan the troop movements at a forthcoming farewell service; A and B companies would enter in single file and sit to the left (north) of the nave, C and D ditto and to the right (south), and so on and so on…

'Hymns?' said a cleric.

' "I Vow to Thee my Country"?' I suggested.

'Not in *A & M*,' said the cleric, 'but in the *Clarendon Hymn Book*. Not popular with the ecclesiastical policymakers these days, because of imperialist and bellicose tendencies. Still, I can arrange to have it printed in the order of service, at the risk of a row I shall very much enjoy.'

'I'm afraid I must deny you the pleasure,' said Malcolm. 'The CO has given me a list of hymns for this service: "All Things Bright and Beautiful", "For All the Saints" and "O God our Help in Ages Past".'

'Appropriate,' said the cleric, 'except possibly for the first, but that's quite inoffensive. By the way, these days we do not sing the verse,

> The rich man in his castle,
>   The poor man at his gate,
> He made them high or lowly,
>   And ordered their estate.'

'Why not?' I enquired.

'It is considered to be undemocratic.'

'Who ever supposed God was a democrat?'

The cleric chuckled. 'The Church is encouraging Him to take populist views,' he said.

'The CO,' said Malcolm, rather wearily, 'does not take populist views. He said he hoped that we should be singing the entire hymn, including the verse you would like to exclude.'

'We *shall* exclude it,' said the cleric.

'Oh dear. My CO says that they always sung that verse when he was at school, that he has cherished memories. Surely, if you could have smuggled in "I Vow to Thee my Country" in the face of official disapprobation, you could manage "The rich man in his castle"?'

' "I Vow to Thee" is mistrusted but not yet forbidden. The verse, "The rich man in his castle" – though the rest of the hymn is of course all right – is definitely forbidden. We have our orders. Lieutenant-Colonel Smith will understand that, I dare say.'

'And I dare say he won't,' said Malcolm to me, as we walked across the cathedral close to his shagged-out Austin. 'He regards this as our service and therefore to be arranged to his liking.'

'It is somebody else's cathedral.'

'Not when *our* service is going on inside it.'

'Oh, come, come. Anyway, I should have thought he would be only too pleased to have those verses left out. He's always complaining about being poor.'

'It comforts him to think that his poverty is ordained. That way he needn't feel inferior.'

'Benghazi' Malcolm (so called because he had won a Military Cross there, leading his platoon into the attack with his bottom bare, during a bad bout of enteritis) now lowered his celebrated bum into the driving seat and opened the passenger door, in a shower of rust and splinters, for me.

'He has nothing much to feel inferior about,' I said. 'Many men are poor, whether or not it is ordained by God.'

'He needs constant assurances on the point – which he doesn't always get. He likes to think that all his officers are poor. But some of them aren't and few of you behave as if you were. Of course, he's much too sensible to try to enforce his views in the mess. But that wouldn't stop him from enforcing them, by way of compensation, elsewhere. This hymn business. Yes, it's someone else's cathedral but it's our recruiting area (that's why we're having the service here) and the occasion is in our honour.'

'Oh God. Poor Malcolm. What shall you do?'

'Tell him that the Bishop has asked him, as a special favour, to allow that verse to be omitted. The idea that his authority is recognised and his permission is being sought will probably render him amenable.'

And so it did. Things did not go so smoothly in the matter of the boots.

I should explain that our troopship was about the last to sail. Air transport was now generally used: it got everyone there much quicker and so did not allow whole divisions of men to hang around doing nothing but sun themselves, for weeks on end, at Her Majesty's expense. But for whatever reasons, nobody was in much hurry to get us to Kenya; HMT *Kitchener of Khartoum* was scheduled to make one more voyage to Mombasa and back before being scrapped, and we were to travel on it. All the officers were delighted and purchased much superior fiction to beguile the journey. The CO alone was furious.

'He has developed a minor frenzy,' Malcolm told me, 'for what he calls "getting on with the job". I'm rather worried about it – it's a phrase which has only come up during the last few days. I think the Colonel of the regiment has been nagging at him.'

'Oh dear.'

'It's all the fault of people like you. You all *enjoyed* yourselves too much in Germany. Now, the Colonel of the regiment rather approves of enjoyment – *his* kind of enjoyment, polo and hunting and trekking and the rest. He does not approve of *your* sort of enjoyment, long weekends at Baden-Baden or Bad Homburg. Since he cannot actually rebuke you for this, he's invented a complaint that "the officers in BAOR did not get on with the job". And now he's using it to torture our new CO.'

'Poor Cuth.'

'The immediate point is that lounging around for four weeks on the *Kitchener of Khartoum* is certainly not "getting on with the job" and the CO is desperate to find ways of using the time to good purpose. The first bother is going to be the matter of ammunition boots.'

The poor bloody infantry wear, or then wore, heavy 'ammunition boots' with blancoed gaiters. Everyone hated this style of dress and wore shoes instead whenever possible. On troopships shoes were always worn in order not to ruin the wooden decks or damage delicate fittings.

'Colonel Cuth,' said Malcolm, 'thinks that if none of the troops wear boots for a month, their feet will get soft. That, you will readily understand, is not "getting on with the job". He intends that all ranks of our battalion shall wear ammunition boots for at least two hours every day…and this despite the copy of standing orders which we have already received from the OC troops of the *Kitchener*. These state, unequivocally, that although troops can embark and disembark in boots, as they must, they will not wear them at any other time for the entire duration of the voyage. There is also another item, stating that there is a compulsory siesta for all ranks on board every afternoon between 1400 and 1600 hours.'

'Siestas are very slack indeed. They even stopped having them in India. Someone said they were an insult to the war effort.'

'That chasm I shall cross,' said our gallant Adjutant, 'when we arrive at it. The CO has not yet noticed the order about siestas; he is still stuck at the paragraph about not wearing ammunition boots. He is determined to appeal against it – has already done so, although there are still several days before we embark. The OC troops has simply written a one-line letter which refers Cuth to the standing orders in force on the matter.'

'From what I remember, the OC troops will only be a lieutenant-colonel, like Cuth.'

'He is vastly senior. The OC troops is like a master of a college used to be. He only gives up when he is carried off. And apart from being senior, the OC troops is paramount on board his ship. If he says no boots, it means *no boots*.'

'Thank God for that.'

'So you may say. But think of me. I shall have to handle the rumpus, which is going to begin the minute we have sailed out of Liverpool. I shall be go-between. I shall have to find some compromise, otherwise Cuth will fret himself to death.'

'What is the OC troops like?'

'He is an extremely amiable old gentleman – so it is reported to me – who lives entirely for his stamp collection. He deprecates any avoidable noise or activity on board his troopship. He loathes any kind of enthusiasm, military or other.'

'What a blissful man. If only *he* could be our CO.'

'Let's have a little loyalty. There's nothing much the matter with Cuth.'

'Probably not. Hymns are a harmless field of obsession. Boots are just that much more damaging, as boots are hard and heavy and disturb the peace. What we have to watch out for,' I said, 'is an ascending scale of unpleasantness. If each obsession is less sympathetic than the last…'

'The next one will probably be the siesta. I don't think that can be too disagreeable.'

'No? Suppose he commands the whole battalion to stay awake?'

'It is time you went back,' said the Adjutant, 'to supervising the packing of your company stores. That is what the Second-in-Command of a company is for. Not for hanging about and making subversive remarks.'

'Had we better take some empty hay boxes?'

'What for?'

'For packing the company's boots in. You know – Not Wanted on Voyage.'

'Piss off,' said Malcolm.

My hero.

My hero was a worried man when I saw him six days later, on a rough morning on the *Kitchener of Khartoum*, twenty-four hours out of Liverpool.

'Colonel Cuth is driving the OC troops crazy,' he told me. 'He won't give the old man any peace to sort out the new stamps he's just bought in London. Cuth says to his face that if our feet grow soft and give out in the jungle, it's going to be *his* fault.'

'Surely,' I said, 'the whole point is that we don't wear ammunition boots in the jungle. We wear jungle boots, which are soft boots with rubber soles. It's those the men have got to get their feet used to. Now I'm absolutely sure that the OC troops will not mind our chaps' going round in canvas boots with rubber soles.'

'*Christ*,' yelled Malcolm. 'Why has no one thought of that?'

When I saw him next, at lunch, he was looking like one of the Eumenides.

'Something wrong?'

'Yes. Cuth says that the men's feet have got to remain used to ammunition boots because they'll be wearing them for routine parades in Nairobi. They may even, says Cuth, be needed for a bit of a show in Mombasa.'

'Obsessions are not to be dispelled by reason,' said O., joining the conversation unasked. 'However, Raven tells me you got over that difficulty about the hymn at Hereford by making it *appear* that Cuth was absolutely entitled to his own way but would give great pleasure if he graciously abrogated his right. Same technique possible here?'

'No. He knows, this time, that he is not entitled to his own way,' Malcolm said. 'He knows that the OC troops outranks him and that the standing orders are exactly what one would expect to find on any troopship. He also knows that he, Cuth Smith, is *right*. The men's feet must be kept hard by constant wearing of ammunition boots, whatever standing orders may say to the contrary and no matter how much trouble may be caused. There'll be no softsoaping him as there was about that hymn.'

'Surely,' said our point-to-point rider, who had drifted up, 'the men could carry their boots up to one of the higher decks, thus making no noise and causing no damage, put down blankets when they get there, and then put on their boots and sit in them, presumably keeping their feet hard.'

'Cuth wants them to move about in their boots. Feet don't keep hard just with sitting in them.'

'I know,' said O. 'They could do exercises in their boots – exercises in which their feet did not touch the deck. Lying on their backs "bicycling", that kind of thing.'

'It's an idea,' said Malcolm. 'Thank you all for taking such an interest. I'll put it to the CO after lunch.'

The weather worsened and everyone except the sailors and the OC troops (seasoned) was sick. Cuth was sick but would not lie down, which meant that Malcolm couldn't lie down either. At the high point of his queasiness he was informed that the OC troops could not approve O.'s idea about exercises, as the booted feet might accidentally strike the deck and so do it damage.

'I said they would strike the blankets on the deck,' said Malcolm, reporting the conference later that evening when the wind had dropped. 'The OC troops said that a lot of harm could be done to a deck with the heel of an ammunition boot, even through an army blanket. But at last they've agreed something. Cuth said that if they built up piles of their kit – shirts, pants and so on – on their blankets, then their boots would strike a good foot of soft material and couldn't possibly damage anything. The OC troops was compelled to agree. So tomorrow the men will proceed, by shifts, to the stern deck, carrying their boots, and will put down their blankets and protective piles of clothes, don their boots, and exercise their legs and feet in the air and over the piles. Brilliant.'

Well, yes. Foolproof, one would have thought, had it not been that, of the first squad that exercised on the stern deck, five men impaled their lower legs on needles in their 'housewives' (repair kits), which had been included in their heaps of clothes to build them up higher, while seven toppled over while 'bicycling', in two cases inflicting huge scars on the deck, in two more cases savagely kicking the skulls of comrades in front or behind and in three cases nearly emasculating personnel sideways adjacent. The damage to the deck was somehow disguised from the ship's crew by our battalion carpenter (summoned in secret), but the damage to skulls and groins could not be disguised from our medical officer, a jolly, gambly, foul-mouthed Liverpudlian lieutenant, who had joined us in Lichfield.

'Mary, Jesus and Joseph,' said the Liverpudlian lieutenant, 'what sort of a loony outfit are you running here?'

'The CO,' I said, gritting my teeth, 'is determined that the men should wear their boots during the voyage and move their feet about inside them. Hence these exercises on the stern deck. *Please* don't try to get it changed. Someone will only think of something even sillier.'

'Could they not be less crowded?'

'No. There would not be time to get through the whole battalion daily.'

'Well,' said the doctor cheerfully, 'if they go on injuring themselves at this rate, it should clear the deck for you very nicely. You do realise,' he went on, 'that when we get to the Red Sea we can't have them lying out there? The sun would kill them.'

'That,' I said, 'would solve a lot of problems.'

The doctor chuckled.

'I'm sorry to disappoint you,' he said, 'but my professional conscience will come into play in their protection somewhere about Suez. Someone had better warn the CO.'

'You'll have *his* professional conscience to cope with.'

'You'd better remind him,' said the doctor, looking very Liverpudlian, 'that in such cases the MO's recommendation is final.'

'Oh, yes. It's just that you may be surprised by the quality and obduracy of the CO's resistance if he doesn't like your recommendation.'

'Why shouldn't he like it? He wouldn't want his men to get heat stroke.'

'No. But he may persuade himself that they need training in how to endure extreme heat.'

'He must understand common sense.'

'He's full of common sense over most things. With a bit of luck he will be over this. We've got a good ten days to Suez. Let's just wait and see.'

'Let's do that,' said the Lieutenant. 'Are you on for a game of backgammon?'

'At 1100 hours?'

'You're in here consulting with me. No one will come in. Lance-Corporal Beatty,' he called. 'You there, Flossie?'

'Thir?' said a voice from an outer office or waiting room.

'I'm not to be disturbed for half an hour. If anybody calls, say I'm busy designing St. Paul's.'

'*Thir?*'

'Famous clerihew, you illiterate slut.'

'All right, thir. That'th what I'll thay. It will be interethting to thee what happenth next.'

'Only a joke, Flossie. Just say I'm on my rounds.'

'On your roundth where…thir?'

'Ship's hygiene.'

'That'th for the ship'th MO.'

'Say I've gone with him, under instruction.'

'And if anyone checkth up?'

'He won't let me down. He owes me a fiver which he hasn't paid. Silly arse,' he said to me as he produced an expensive travelling backgammon set and a bottle of Irish whiskey from a drawer. 'He bet me five quid that Labour would win the general election.' (This was the summer of 1955.) 'Said the people were sound at heart. Couldn't understand that one dose of socialist humbuggery and busybodying puts everyone off for a good ten years. Ten shillings a point, right?'

The CO was not very pleased about the large number of soldiers declared unfit for further 'deck exercise', but like many men of obsession he was prepared to relax slightly in practice once he had vanquished in principle and been given his way, or a good part of it. Anyhow, by now he had a new craze to occupy

him. As Malcolm and I had surmised, he most strongly
deprecated the ship's regulation which enjoined on all a two-
hour siesta between 1400 and 1600 hours. He therefore started
badgering the OC troops for permission to conduct special
officers' seminars in the ship's library during those hours. There
would be no noise, he said: nobody would be disturbed.

'Except,' said the OC troops (Malcolm reporting), 'for your
officers. I dare say they like a siesta as well as anybody.'

'My officers,' said Cuth, 'are my concern. They all know
they've got to get on with the job.'

'What particular job had you in mind?'

'Beating the Mau Mau.'

'The Mau Mau,' said the OC troops, 'are already beaten. Do
for God's sake get the thing right. You are not going to war
against an enemy; you are going to Kenya to help clean the
place up. You are going to collect out of the forest a few
hundred starving and syphilitic wrecks armed with catapults
and put them in detention camps until the administration
decides on the most humane way of treating them.'

'I won't argue with you, Colonel,' said Cuth, 'though some
might put the matter in a different perspective. Whatever we are
doing in the forest, we shall need certain basic skills.'

'Not the sort you can learn in the ship's library.'

'I beg your pardon, Colonel,' said the courteous Cuth. 'We
can learn Swahili in your library. Surely a useful asset?'

Game, set and match to Colonel Cuth, as Malcolm told us
later. Further objections from the OC troops would have been
merely perverse.

However, Colonel Cuth now proceeded to overdo it.
Narked, if not very much, by the numbers of soldiers excused
from taking part in deck exercises with ammunition boots, he
decided on a little compensation. All officers, he promulgated,
besides wearing boots when on the stern deck with their men
(and thus being compelled to keep order from a squatting or at
best sitting position), would also bring their boots with them to

the ship's library every day and wear them during the Swahili lessons from 1400 to 1600 hours. In order to prevent their damaging the library floor, subalterns would bring piles of clobber of the kind they took on deck, while captains and above (whose dignity would suffer if they were seen to be toting laundry about) would use books from the library shelves to put their booted feet on.

Before the first day of the Swahili lessons, it had become apparent that there was only one Swahili book on the ship, an out-of-date concordance which belonged to the senior steward. A list of suitable words was copied out of this on to a worm-eaten blackboard by the officers i/c Swahili (O., and a rather precious but very intelligent National Service second lieutenant who had just come down from Oxford); the arrangement was approved (there being no better) by the Colonel; and after everyone had put on boots and, in the case of captains and above, rested his feet on volumes from the shelves, O. requested the CO's permission to begin.

'One moment,' said the CO, surveying the class. 'I see that the medical officer is not present.'

'The custom is, sir,' said Malcolm carefully, 'that the MO does not attend parades of regimental officers unless specifically requested to do so.'

'Why not?'

'He has private studies to attend to, sir. We are asked to take note that a medical officer, like any doctor in practice, has to keep up with current trends in medicine and important new theories, forensic and pathological. He therefore has a lot of reading to do, sir – '

' – And plenty of time in which to do it. He spent three hours yesterday after dinner playing bridge, so no doubt he is not pressed, at the moment, for leisure in which to pursue his studies. Will the orderly officer of the day kindly find Lieutenant Wosking and request his presence here?'

After about ten minutes, a very cross Dr Wosking, who had been hauled out of his bunk, reported to the ship's library, was sent back to his quarters to get his boots and also, as he ranked only as a lieutenant, a suitable pile of shirts to rest his feet on. As the Colonel pointed out, when Wosking was finally settled, he would need to know Swahili as well as the rest of us.

The plain fact remained that his legitimate, or at least his customary, prerogative had been denied. A medical officer does not wear boots, not even, unless he chooses to, in the field. The medical officer does not attend officers' parades, for PT, say, or instruction, unless there is a very special reason and he is warned well in advance.

'The CO was out of order,' said our point-to-point rider that evening.

'He's been well paid out,' said Malcolm. 'After the Swahili lesson, Wosking went straight to the ship's librarian and told him of the use his books were being put to by captains and above. The librarian (a steward of long standing) has complained (a) that this is vandalism and (b) that damage has already been done, to covers and bindings, to the extent of £57 17s 9 ¾ d. The OC troops has directed Colonel Cuth to find the money, not out of any regimental fund, but out of his own pocket. Now, before you all start chortling yourselves sick, please remember that Lieutenant-Colonel Cuth Smith is indeed a poor man, with two growing boys to educate; also that he genuinely and conscientiously believes that he has the battalion's interest and honour at heart. Remember, too, that it is your duty, and should be your pleasure, to support your commanding officer with all the loyalty you can muster. In short,' said Malcolm rather splendidly, 'I expect to see more willingness, keenness and cooperation, and less scrimshanking and girlish giggling, from all of you. Colonel Cuth is a very good-natured and well-intentioned officer; and if he is, on occasion, rather misguided in his enthusiasms, you will not stop him by thwarting or opposing him, you will merely make him unhappy and very possibly bloody-minded.'

'Which is all very well,' said O. after Malcolm had moved heavily away, 'provided Colonel Cuth confines his compulsive hankerings to trivial matters. What happens if something really serious crops up and he starts riding his romping hobby-horse then?'

'Malcolm will manage him,' I said. 'As I understand it, the technique with Cuth is now to give way over things that don't matter in order to keep him in his normal good temper. The more he thinks we're on his side, the less he'll push his luck when he knows we're against him.'

'Wrong,' said the point-to-point rider. 'He does not acknowledge opposition when he gets carried away. As we know, every now and then something carries him away. Most things he will discuss as calmly and as rationally as you please. He made excellent sense the other day when he sent for me to talk about the regimental saddle club he wants to establish in Nairobi. Very slow he was, but also friendly and amenable to argument. But there are some things about which he knows that, whatever anyone else may know, he knows best. So far, thank God, these have only been trifling things like ammunition boots and siestas. But when such things appear on the agenda, as we have all observed, he is simply non-negotiable...as the moneylender said of the cheque which came back marked "no account".'

'I'd still back Malcolm to negotiate with him over anything that really mattered.'

'Perhaps,' said O. 'The trouble is that Malcolm is getting no practice.'

'I should have thought,' I said, 'that he was getting plenty.'

'Only,' insisted our amateur jockey, 'about small things. He will need lots of special practice before he can cope with the Queen of Spades.'

'Do you remember that absurd but endearing film?' I said. 'A Russian officer of engineers made a huge sum playing cards with some guardees by naming the Queen of Spades as next card to turn up. He'd been tipped off by a ghost played by Edith Evans.'

'There'll come no ghost played by Edith Evans to tip Malcolm off in time,' said O.

'In the film the face of the card suddenly changes in front of them all – so the engineer hadn't won after all and went mad as a result. The card changes back again, just as they're all putting him in the loony van, so nobody sees it.'

'That's another thing,' said our horseman. 'Serious matters are apt to go into flux under your eyes. Which is no help at all.'

'Everything is in flux, according to Heraclitus,' I said, 'and in that case nothing can matter at all.'

'That's the same as saying that in the long run we'll all be dead,' said O. 'In the army it's the short run we have to deal with – the here and now.'

'Here and now,' said Malcolm, who was very restless that evening and had just rejoined us, 'there is another cauldron about to bubble.'

'So long as it doesn't set the house on fire.'

'One or two people may be scalded. The CO has caused continuing schedules to be published in tomorrow's orders about the use of the stern deck for boot exercises. This schedule takes us all the way to Mombasa. I have just whispered in his ear that it might be ill advised to have men on the stern deck at noon when, say, we were stuck in the Suez Canal. He says that they must learn to get on with the job no matter what the weather.'

'You'd better watch out for the MO,' I said. 'He's worried about that too.'

'How do we get the MO on our side?' said Malcolm. 'I mean, make a chum of him? We're going to need his help.'

'First, you apologise to him for what happened the other day about that Swahili lesson.'

'If I do, I shall have to tell him that he needn't attend any more. Cuth insists that he should.'

'Invent a man who's ill enough to require constant attention. That'll cover it.'

'If one of our men were that ill,' said Malcolm, 'Cuth would be the first in the sickbay – even if the man had bubonic plague – to wish him well and ask what he could do for him. We'd look pretty silly inventing a sick man and then being unable to produce him.'

'Take the doctor into your confidence,' said O., characteristically at his most sensible when others were at their silliest. 'Explain about Cuth's little urges. Make the doctor feel like one of the club. He'll be your man then.'

And so he was. He settled the matter of the stern deck quite simply by asking Cuth to let him cover his own professional reputation by persuading the ship's crew to put up awnings in the Suez Canal and the Red Sea. Cuth magnanimously consented. The doctor was liked by the crew, because he had run a starting-price book on the Derby a few days before and manfully paid out despite some very stiff wagers on a popular winner. Awnings? they said. Of course. Much easier than a boxing ring, which was rather a finicking affair.

Boxing ring?

On the bow deck, under the bridge. It had to be there because that's where the necessary brackets and fittings were.

Yes, yes, said Lieutenant Wosking. He understood all that. But who had ordered the boxing competition?

Lieutenant-Colonel Smith, they said, for his battalion. And who was the boxing officer? Wosking enquired. Someone called Raven, they said: he'd been round to inspect the ropes for the ring.

'Yes, yes,' I said, when Wosking collared me about this. 'I am indeed the battalion boxing officer. And I have a darling little certificate of proficiency on the strength of a course I was sent on.'

'What sort of course?'

'Four days at Hamelin. The Pied Piper place. Charming town.'

'And on the strength of four days' instruction there you propose to run a battalion boxing competition?'

'Why not? I did it in Germany.'

'Didn't your MO get into a state?'

'He did rather. There have been a number of nasty accidents lately.

'Some of them fatal. More in the last two months before we left England. I do read some of the literature which comes round for army doctors. If there are any accidents on board this ship, I shall be in for it. So will you.'

'And so will the Colonel,' I said. 'Shall we suggest that the competition be scrapped? We can say there is all the more chance of an accident on a ship. A sudden lurch, anything like that... A boxer slips and hits his head on a coil of steel cable... Do they still have burials at sea, or would they freeze the chap till Mombasa?'

'Take care you're not laughing on the other side of your face,' said Wosking.

'Well,' I said, 'we'd better go to the CO and warn him – if you think we ought.'

'I do.'

But Colonel Cuth was going to have his boxing. No problem about heat, he said. The best time for the boxing was the early evening and since the boat would be going West the bow would be out of the sun. Accidents? Of course there had been accidents and would be again. One couldn't spend one's life cancelling things because of the possibility of accidents. Since this was a proposition with which, though I should have been happy to escape the trouble of the thing, I very much agreed, I couldn't fault him there. I could only remind him, as did Wosking, that we must take very careful precautions and that I would be needing a lot of responsible officers and NCOs as umpires and seconds and assistants to ensure nothing went wrong. Quite right, Colonel Cuth said. The doctor still regarded it as not right at all, but he too acknowledged that one could not put off what might be a highly entertaining event (by that stage of the voyage we all needed entertainment) just in case something went wrong.

'Have you got the OC troops' permission, Colonel?' the doctor said.

Colonels of infantry battalions like to be called 'sir'. They regard 'Colonel' as casual, cavalry usage. Cuth Smith was no exception.

'Call me "sir",' he said sharply. (A mistake, thought I.) 'The OC troops is agreeable providing no applause is allowed during the rounds. Standard practice, I believe.'

I nodded.

'And no women are allowed as spectators. Also standard practice?'

'Not any more, sir, I'm sorry to say. Women have been allowed as spectators since last autumn. And a very improper audience they sometimes make.'

The Colonel, as a matter of chivalry, now changed his ground.

'On board this ship,' he said, 'the only ladies are four wives of senior officers.'

'None of them officers of our regiment, sir. There is no reason why their wom – their wives should wish to attend.'

'I can think of several,' said the MO, and grinned louchely.

'That's enough from both of you,' said Colonel Smith. 'It is all quite clear. If army boxing regulations allow the presence of females, then the ladies aboard should be invited to attend, if only out of courtesy to their husbands. They are not of a class who will applaud in a vulgar fashion…nor of a type' – he looked at the doctor – 'who will take an unwholesome delight in the proceedings. This said, I shall take it, Mr Raven, that you have no objection to their being present.'

'None, sir. So long as they clearly understand that no noise may be made while a round is being fought. Women…even ladies…are apt to be carried away. You are familiar, sir, with what Martial and others have to say about their behaviour in the Colosseum?'

'You know very well that I have not had your advantages at Cambridge and elsewhere. Do not patronise me, Mr Raven. Simply get on with the job.'

So I did. Together with the battalion carpenter I checked the ring and its fittings – five times. I chose a cadre of officers and senior NCOs to act as judges (I myself, as boxing officer, would have to be referee), timekeepers, marshals of the audience, administrators of first aid, cleaners and keepers of the ring. Suitable contestants were chosen, weighed, medically examined, dentally inspected, and given brief refresher courses in the noble art by PT instructors and myself. The contestants in each weight were numbered, their names drawn, the lists made, duplicated in the orderly room, despatched to all officials and displayed in public places.

So far, so good.

And then came a summons to the Adjutant's office.

'The CO wants to know,' said Malcolm, 'why no officers are taking part in the boxing.'

'They are taking a huge part. They are judging, timing, organising, seconding –'

'– The CO wants to know why none of them is actually boxing.'

Count up to ten.

'It never occurred to me that any of them should. Officers do not normally take part because any of them with any knowledge of the sport are needed to judge and so on. Those with no knowledge are needed to organise and arrange. Apart from that,' I said, 'you know as well as I do that to put officers in the ring against other Ranks is asking for every kind of trouble in the book.'

'The CO does not think so.'

'The last CO did. We never had officers boxing in Göttingen and he raised no objection.'

'We are talking about the present CO. Lieutenant-Colonel Smith. He wants to see at least four junior officers in the ring – boxing.'

'Then perhaps he would care to run the competition himself.'

'Don't be insolent.'

'Malcolm. When officers box with Other Ranks, one of three things happens. Either there is a fair and sporting bout, at which everyone is delighted – though even then, if the officer is awarded the match by the judges, there is often grizzling about favouritism. *Or* the officer wins hands down, in which case it is said that a weak opponent was deliberately drawn against him. *Or* the Other Rank wins hands down, sometimes humiliating the officer, in which case there is a lot of ugly glee. In any case whatever, class prejudice and hatred, never far below the surface even in the best of battalions, are awakened and sometimes dangerously roused. Am I right?'

'The CO is asking nothing unusual – a lot of officers box in the Welsh regiments – and certainly nothing contrary to declared policy or existing regulations. Am I right?'

I nodded reluctantly.

'Then kindly go away, Simon, and arrange that a minimum of four subalterns should take part in the boxing.'

'Very well, sir. It will mean scrapping and redrafting these lists, which have taken time to prepare. It will mean selecting four willing and suitable officers, which may not be easy. It will mean finding and briefing new and obviously less adequate people to take on many of the offices on which the success of the thing depends. It could mean, in one word, disaster. I wish to go on record, *now*, as saying so.'

'Please don't make difficulties, Simon. I have rather more than I can easily bear.'

'Oh. I see. I'm sorry, Malcolm. I've been self-important and silly about this whole thing. I'll do what is asked and bother you no more. Cubs' honour.'

'That's my good boy.'

My hero.

Soon afterwards, I reported to O. and the jockey what Malcolm had said about having more difficulties than he could easily bear.

'It can't all be Cuth's doing,' I said.

'It isn't,' said O. 'It's the instructions which keep coming in on the ship's radio from the GOC-in-C's headquarters. It seems that the minute we arrive we're to be pitched straight into some major operation.'

'I thought,' said the point-to-point man, 'that we were simply waiting for the Mau Mau to come out of the jungle and then intern them.'

'They're not coming out quick enough,' said O., who always knew about that kind of thing. 'Too many of our troops tied down and doing nothing but waiting. They want to flush out all the remaining Mau Mau from the Aberdare Forest in one final operation and then run down the number of units in Kenya. The Government is keen on saving money.'

'But what form,' I enquired, 'is this operation to take? They can't expect us to disembark and plunge straight into the jungle without some preliminary training.'

'The talk is,' said O., 'that we shall only be required to provide ambushes. Heavy guns and bombers will plaster the Aberdare Forest; out will come the Mau Mau; and our ambushes will capture them.'

'Capture?'

'The policy is that from now on Mau Mau terrorists are to be fired on only if they resist arrest.'

'But what happens if they fire first? They have still got a few pukka firearms left, or so I'm told.'

'If they fire first,' said O., 'that's just too bad. Politicians require that we set a humanitarian example.'

'So prudence dictates,' I said, 'unless one wishes to risk perishing for the humanitarian ideals of politicians, that the minute one sees a Mau Mau contingent one shoots the lot. One can then say, without risk of refutation, that they were either about to fire or to resist with other weapons. They have a lot of things called pangas, which resemble very sharp and nasty short-swords.'

'There is now a new and special kind of magistrate,' said O., 'recruited in England, that goes round investigating the deaths of terrorists. If they can prove we have killed a Mau Mau without provocation, we're in real trouble.'

'But if the Mau Mau in question is already dead,' I insisted, 'our story is the only one and the magistrate has to believe it.'

'Presumably.'

'If everyone's getting so humane all of a sudden,' the jockey said, 'why are they allowing the jungle to be strafed and bombed?'

'It has been conceded by the politicians, with their fingers no doubt crossed behind their backs, that the Mau Mau still in the forest are in such miserable case that we are doing them a good turn by forcing them out, even if one or two are killed in the process. But once they are out, it's got to be, "Dear Mr Mau Mau, kindly come this way." '

'That's what our ambushes will be doing?' I said.

'Right,' said O.

'Then no wonder Malcolm is in a state. The idea of sending untrained men to set up ambushes in a totally strange and very formidable environment…and telling them that they must not fire unless fired upon…it's an absurdity. What does the CO think?'

'He thinks we must get on with the job,' said O. 'I don't think he's really taken it in, about not killing "the enemy", as he sees them. He thinks we're going into old-fashioned action. Which is one more worry for Malcolm.'

'Of course, what nobody seems to understand,' said O., who had fought with some distinction in Korea a few years before, 'is that bombing forests and so on never brings out the people you want. They go to ground, quite easily. You get a few animals coming out in a panic – but not many even of them, unless the bombardment is very intensive. The Aberdare Forest is too large for intensive bombardment and I suspect that our resources are pretty meagre. So the odds are that nothing and nobody will come out at all.'

'Tell Malcolm that. It might cheer him up.'

'I have. But he's got another horrid worry. The VD returns.'

'VD is always with us.'

'Precisely. Some six cases have been diagnosed since we've been at sea,' said O. 'Four of clap and two of the great pox. Clearly they were picked up in England before we sailed.'

'Quite a virtuous statistic. I remember,' said the amateur rider, 'when we had thirty-three cases, in Göttingen, in a single month.'

'*Thirty-three?*'

'Yes. I've always remembered it, because thirty-three is my favourite number at roulette. Compared with that, six cases since we've sailed is, as Ronald Searle would say, a Kredit to the Skol.'

'They take,' said O., 'a very strict view of VD in Kenya. It is assumed, if you catch it, that you have been out of bounds to a brothel area.'

'Why shouldn't you have caught it from a settler's beautiful daughter?'

'White women in Kenya don't have VD.'

'Baronness Blixen did.'

'She'd have been far too grand to give it to a common soldier. No. If one of our soldiers has the pox or the clap, he's had it from a black when out of bounds. That is axiomatic, as far as the authorities are concerned, the absolute truth that needs no proving. It follows that he must be courtmartialled, found guilty and sentenced to a month or more in a military prison.'

'A month in the slammer for a dose of clap. *Not* very humane.'

'That,' said O., 'is what is worrying Malcolm. He says that when our six cases get to Kenya, they'll be courtmartialled as a matter of course.'

'Surely not – if they caught what they caught in England.'

'Malcolm has been advised, by a senior officer on this boat, that that will not be taken into account. It is a matter of handing out "deterrent sentences". Soldiers in Kenya with VD must be given "deterrent sentences" to discourage the rest. If you make an exception, for whatever reason, the exception will be known about but probably not the reason. Other soldiers may conclude that a reign of clemency is coming in, which may make for lax behaviour, and then for bloody-mindedness when that behaviour is punished as brutally as ever. So our six wretches can expect no mercy. Malcolm is a just man and is badly bothered.'

'By the time we get to Kenya,' said our jockey, 'they should have been cured…if Doctor Wosking knows what he's at.'

'He does. And he's very much an ally. But the records are there. They will be inspected by some senior medic shortly after our arrival.'

'Oh, no, they won't,' said Doctor Wosking, who had just turned up with his backgammon set. 'Dear little Flossie got up an accidental fire and it just so happened that some of the records were burnt. Since we're at sea, no one else has yet had a copy. However, there isn't much gratitude in the world. One of your men has complained that Flossie has been carrying on in the lay. Your man is called Stevens, J H.'

'Mine,' said O. 'I'll settle him. He's a thief. It's always men like that who get righteous about club members.'

'Club members?'

'Boys like your Flossie.'

'Not Flossie, for Christ's sake.'

'Your Lance-Corporal Clerk.'

'That's better.'

'Have you,' I said, 'told the Adjutant the good news — about the files going up in smoke?'

'Yes. I've just seen him. He says that that's one problem out of the way. And would I ask Simon Raven to step into his office as soon as he's finished his mid-morning coffee? Boxing, he says.'

'But we've settled all that,' I said. 'I've agreed to do everything the CO wants and I'm doing it — though not for the CO's sake but for Malcolm's. I'll pop along and reassure the old thing. He needs all the reassurance he can get.'

'Second Lieutnant Richard Legh,' Malcolm said. 'What do you know about him?'

'He came down from Oxford last year with a First in Greats. He received a National Service commission in the usual way, though his training was shortened because he'd been in some university cadet set-up at Oxford. He joined us soon after we went into barracks at Lichfield, i.e., about five weeks before we sailed. He seems an agreeable and highly intelligent fellow, and he is helping O. with the Swahili.'

'A little bit affected?'

'Not bad as Oxonians go.'

'A little bit conceited?'

'Not everyone gets a First in Greats.'

'And of course far too privileged a young gentleman to be made to box in your competition?'

'What on earth do you mean? He's wholly unsuitable. He has legs like the stems of hock glasses and a chest like the handle of a broomstick.'

'He was found fit for active service in the infantry. The CO thinks he is fit enough to box and does not see that an Oxford degree excuses him.'

'Nor does it. But I've already put *five* young officers into the new lists. Surely enough?'

'The CO is very keen that Richard Legh should box.'

'I suppose he wants Richard Legh brought down a peg?'

'He didn't say so. He just said that he could not understand why he had been left out of the boxing.'

'Because he has a lot to do preparing the Swahili lessons. Because he has never boxed in his life. Because he would be an embarrassment in the ring. Because no decent man could bear to hit such an obvious muff. Look, Malcolm. When we did our course at Hamelin, they said it was important to use judgement and instinct to make sure that certain soldiers did not get into the boxing ring. You'll know them when you see them, the senior instructor said: just don't let them box. And another thing he said, very emphatically, Malcolm, was: "Always remember, the final decision is yours. If you are required to organise a boxing competition, you are responsible for seeing that the wrong people don't get mixed up in it. *You*, the organiser, have the last word."

'So this time I'm having the last word, Malcolm. No Richard Legh in my boxing ring.'

'The CO won't like it.'

'Legh is like…a brittle beanpole. As I just said, no decent man could bear to hit him. If through bad luck he drew another kind of man, he'd be half killed. I'd almost certainly have to stop the fight. Fiasco or carnage: is that really what the CO wants?'

'He wants Richard Legh in the ring. In this regiment, he says, no one is too dainty or distinguished to join in with the men. It's part of getting on with the job.'

'Malcolm…can't you get round him?'

'No. I've tried. He is determined. If you stand on your rights as boxing officer, he will either overrule you – '

' – He can't – '

' – or he will make very nasty trouble for you. There are some subtle ways of punishing officers who stand on their technical rights and give offence to their CO. No one comes forward to help them: they are seen as barrack-room lawyers – subversive and disloyal.'

'What shall I do, Malcolm?'

'What you are told. You can't come to any harm.'

'Richard Legh can. And so can I, whatever you say. *I* am responsible. If something goes wrong, they'll be down on me like a road drill. *They* won't say, he was being loyal to his CO and respecting his wishes. *They* will say, he should have stopped it before it started and he had, as he well knew, every right to do so. Cleft stick. Knight's fork at chess: if I save one piece I lose the other.'

'Simon. You are being very obtuse this morning. Before Legh can box, he must be passed fit by the MO. Do I make myself plain?'

'Right,' said Wosking. 'We should be able to find something wrong with him. Please ask him to come in.'

As boxing officer I had to be present when any boxer was medically examined.

'I'm sorry,' I apologised to Richard Legh. 'Regulations compel me to be here.'

'Why should I mind?'

With that he stripped the khaki shirt off his narrow torso, eased his slacks over his skeletal knees to his ankles and shoved down his pants to reveal a surprisingly stalwart groin.

'You know,' he said, 'I'm a fitter man than you might think. Otherwise I should hardly have been passed fit to serve abroad with this battalion. I'll tell you another thing. I came fifteenth out of 350 odd in the spring cross country steeplechase at Mons OCTU. So you don't need to worry about me.'

'The question is,' I said, 'whether you're fit to box.'

At a sign from the MO Legh pulled up his pants with huge hands that dangled from arms like twigs.

'I am fit to do anything, within reason, that I am required to do. If you want another officer for your boxing, here am I, take me.'

'I don't want another officer for my boxing. I shall only have to change the draw, for your weight, for the second time. The CO wants you to box. He has an old-fashioned army prejudice about graduates: he thinks we're soft.'

'Funny,' reflected Richard Legh. 'In the old days the army took a great many regular officers from the universities. What has Colonel Smith got against them?'

'He was a poor boy, relatively speaking, who came to the army straight from school. He thinks that people who spend three or four years reading Latin and Greek are pampered.'

'Then it's up to me to show him he's wrong.'

'Richard,' I said. 'You know nothing about boxing. You're the wrong build and wrong physique. Wosking here can get you out of it by finding something wrong with you. Even a loose tooth would be enough.'

'I had a dental check before coming to Lichfield. If the Colonel wants to see me box,' said Richard Legh, 'I shall be happy to oblige him. You read your Plato, I know – I spotted you with a Loeb edition of *The Republic* the other day.'

'What's Plato got to do with it?'

'You may recall Socrates' views about obedience to the state and those in authority under the state. Such obedience is obligatory.'

'Obedience to their legitimate orders or requests. Not to their whims.'

'If a whim is expressed as an order, then it is so. He who indulges his whim will be answerable to the gods: so will he be who refuses to obey an order. I am, as it happens, a Christian: the same sort of reasoning applies. *Mutatis mutandis*, of course.'

You, I thought, are an insufferable prig. If you get hurt, it serves you right.

'Then I prick you – thus,' I said, sticking my pencil into his name, which was entered under 'ineligible'. 'Your weight makes you light welter. Luckily, I now see that I shall have no need to make another draw if I give you a bye in the first round.'

'Is that fair?'

'Someone has got to have a bloody bye,' I grated. 'Why not you? Please don't make any more trouble.'

'Trouble is just what I'm trying not to make.'

'I'm sorry, Richard. It's just that life would have been much simpler for all of us if you'd allowed the doctor here to find a sprain in your little finger or an itch in one of your ears.'

'I dare say. And if I'd had any such affliction I should have been the first to tell you. I haven't and that's all there is to it.'

'So there it is,' I said to Malcolm. 'Just for once we have an honest and an honourable man in our midst. Quite pleased with himself for being so.'

'Over the years,' said Malcolm, 'I have come to dread one thing more than any other.'

'Honest men?'

'No. Honest intellectuals. Why couldn't he be a conscientious objector and skip the army altogether? It's quite easy these days. You just fill in a form when you get your call-up papers.'

'He's not that type. He prides himself on his manliness and normality. He sees nothing wrong in the use of force to defend the state. Boxing, he would probably tell you, is part of the necessary training in quick thinking and agile moving. He's thought about it all and he has come to his conclusions.'

'Intellectually. Which I suppose has made him smug?'

'Almost unbearable.'

'You see what I mean about honest – and honourable – intellectuals. They can't just do something, like anybody else, because it is the done thing. They think it out, they watch themselves thinking it out and give themselves maddening airs when they finally condescend to agree with the rest of us.'

'What is to be done?'

'Nothing. He's had his chance. Now he must take what's coming to him.'

'If he's pummelled to pieces, it may not be good for discipline. People will despise him.'

'Only if you stop the fight. If,' said Malcolm, 'you make him go the full distance, people will admire his courage.'

'Suppose he's knocked out?'

'That wouldn't be too bad. Provided he lasted for a round or two. Who's he up against?'

'The winner of Matthews v. Tarlin. Which has to be Tarlin. He's one of those chunky numbers, short and vibrant. You remember what Byron's boxing coach advised – "Mill to the left and mill to the right"? That's Tarlin.'

'Oh, God. Fur flying everywhere. Like a dog fight.'

'Precisely.'

'I must count my blessings,' said Malcolm. 'Dr Wosking and his clerk have got our VD cases off the hook. As for the CO, his immediate obsession is about Richard Legh and the boxing. Surely, with just a tiny bit of luck it can't turn out too badly?'

It turned out worse than anyone could possibly have imagined. As I had predicted, Tarlin beat Matthews; I had to stop the fight after the first ten seconds of the second round. This meant that Richard Legh must fight Tarlin. 'Mill to the left and mill to the right.' I thought I knew exactly what would happen. Stocky Tarlin would mill at beanpole Legh's midriff; Legh would at first flail ineffectively back, then gradually droop as he was forced nearer and nearer to the ropes, until, as Legh sagged, Tarlin's whirling fists went banging like pistons on his jaw, his mouth, his nose. Very soon Legh would be cruelly scuffed in the cheeks and welling with blood from all orifices. I should have to stop the fight after about half a minute, the men would jeer as the humiliated Legh was manoeuvred out of the ring like a wrecked bicycle, Tarlin would preen and prance, the image of the gloating prole in victory, and would bounce away towards the contestants' entrance/exit while his besotted comrades banged and stamped and (so to speak) threw their sweaty nightcaps in the air. That was my vision and quite nasty enough. The reality, colourless and noiseless, was a monster of horror.

What I should have remembered about Richard Legh was that he was an exceedingly intelligent man who had a very long reach from a very great height. When Tarlin rushed milling left and right towards him, Legh simply stuck out his left arm and stopped Tarlin dead with a straight punch on the nose. Tarlin next attacked with his head down. This time he was stopped by a flimsy but painful (on Tarlin's nose again) uppercut. Tarlin retreated once more, clearly angered, eyes watering. He bent himself nearly double this time, his face and torso far too low for lanky Legh to reach down and administer another uppercut, and simply ran at Legh, still milling, and with his head butting straight towards Legh's parts. Being, as I have explained, too tall in this predicament to uppercut, Legh punched down with his right and landed a foul (rabbit) blow to the back of the neck, not harmful (though it might have been) to the top of the spine, where it struck, but lethal nonetheless, in that it levelled Tarlin very hard on to the deck. This occurred quite silently, as I have written above, because Tarlin's head hit the boards, not with the boney forehead, but with the soft nose (rather prominent on Tarlin's face) which was crushed against and almost right into the wooden surface. Again, the scene was colourless, or almost: white boxing vests and shorts against scrubbed deck; and, to my amazement, no blood.

The first thing to do was to count Tarlin out, which, with the assistance of the timekeeper, I now did. The next thing, as Tarlin showed no sign of stirring, was to call for a stretcher. A rather puzzled Legh, who was leaning over Tarlin to peer at him, was now escorted to his corner by his seconds (two National Service second lieutenants). Three orderlies came into the ring and handled Tarlin through the ropes to the stretcher bearers. An ugly susurration began to rise above the audience, while two bright-eyed women who were sitting with the CO began a fierce and clearly audible argument across his chest about the rights and wrongs of the matter. These were desperately confusing; as referee, I was required to resolve them and give a decision in a matter of little more than moments. Grim and sweaty, I stood in a vacant corner and tried to sort the thing out.

In the first place, there was no question whatever but that Richard Legh had delivered a foul blow. He had more or less thumped down with his fist on to the nape of Tarlin's neck and fouler than that you could not get. And yet it was difficult to see how he could have defended himself otherwise. Tarlin's butting was also foul; it was aimed at Legh's fork, which made it doubly foul; but it had not actually made contact. Had it done so, Tarlin would have been disqualified out of hand, but his head had been a good nine inches short of Legh's *membrum virile* when Legh struck in defence, side-stepping as he did so and thus moving out of the line of the butt. Would he have escaped it altogether if he had not made his downward blow? Could this blow fairly be said to have been aimed at the top of the head (a legitimate target if the head was bowed) and to have missed it through no fault of Legh's? The answer to the first question was that Tarlin's head, had it continued in a right line, would almost certainly have struck Legh's thigh very dangerously on the joint between the limb and the pelvis, for Legh, though side-stepping, was too cumbrous to have escaped altogether. The answer to the second question was that, yes, Legh had punched at such of the legitimate target as was visible and could hardly have been expected to submit to probable and violent injury from an opponent who was in a definitely foul posture and making a deliberately foul attempt.

Another question: why had Tarlin, who knew the rules perfectly well, made this disgraceful sortie? Had he forgotten Legh's height and thought that he was aiming at his opponent's upper belly and not his *privata*? Answer one: Legh's straight left followed by his uppercut must have riled Tarlin beyond bearing – though more because of the loss of face, I thought, than because of the actual pain inflicted. Answer two: even had Tarlin thought that he was butting at Legh's solar plexus and not his *pubes*, he was still totally out of order. Final question: did Tarlin hope to raise his head before reaching Legh and confront him without butting him? Answer: if so, he had left it too late; for had Tarlin raised his head at the time he was struck, he would have been in danger of striking Legh viciously in the midriff (or lower) with his crown; and if he was imagining his opponent as being shorter than Legh, he must have known that he might have savaged that opponent (again with his crown) with the most appalling blow to the face.

And now it was time to pronounce. I looked at the CO, who did not look back. I looked at the chattering women and resolved to have them banned from the next session on the ground of shameless behaviour. I looked at Malcolm, who raised his eyes to Heaven. I saw the absolutely motionless Tarlin disappear on his stretcher through the entrance/exit; I turned my glance to Legh, no longer puzzled but apparently indifferent, who was now sitting on a stool in his corner showing what seemed like five yards of boney thigh, the least lust-making I have ever inspected in my whole life. I listened briefly to the hornet-buzz of the audience. I announced: 'Private Tarlin is disqualified from the bout for a deliberate and very dangerous foul.'

The audience melted away from the bow deck, muttering. Although there were still two bouts to be fought that evening, the only spectators that remained were serjeants, warrant officers, officers and the CO's two female guests. Even a small group of ship's officers, who had been watching with some enjoyment, swiftly dispersed. The verdict of the majority was obvious: Second Lieutenant Legh, being an officer, had been given the fight, though he was more fouling than fouled.

Nor did the MO's verdict improve matters: 'Tarlin is badly shocked; he will have to have surgery on his nose as soon as we reach Mombasa.'

And of course there was another factor in the situation, perhaps the most hellish of all: Richard Legh, having won his bout, would go through to fight another.

The cognoscenti, my own assistants, that is to say, and the better informed PTIs, thought I had been right in my decision. Those concerned more with politics than with boxing took a different view. The Colonel himself did not comment, just went around the ship looking rather hurt, as though somebody had forgotten his birthday. Both O. and the jockey thought that I had had good enough ground to disqualify Legh and should indeed have done so in order to get a dangerous joker out of the game. Malcolm said the whole affair had been brutally difficult, but also opined that a decision in favour of Tarlin would have been well received by the rank and file, though not nearly as well received as the decision in favour of Legh had been badly received.

'In my worst nightmares,' I said, 'I did not envisage Legh's going on to fight a second match.'

'What line does Legh take?' Malcolm said.

'He says he did his best in very troublesome circumstances. I agree. I did not and do not see that he could have done anything else, given that low charge of Tarlin's. That's why I called him as winner.'

'Do you think that Wosking could *now* find something wrong with him? Couldn't he have hurt his hand giving that punch?'

'I've thought of that – and a great many other things. Legh is firm. He didn't much want to fight in the beginning. He was ordered to and of course consented. Once having consented, however, he will proceed by the law. It is a brave and unexceptionable attitude. I hope the Colonel has taken notice of this instance of "pampered" university behaviour. Not many Sandhurst men would have conducted themselves so well.'

'The Colonel thinks his win was a fluke. He thinks you found in favour of Legh because you are another university man.'

'What do the men think? The RSM will have told you.'

'Much the same – with a stronger ingredient of class.'

'They don't think that Tarlin lost his head?'

'You'd better talk to the RSM yourself. He may be able to advise you about the continuation of the business.'

The RSM was a good-spirited father of his flock, a little apt to get flustered and to fluster everyone else, a decent and an upright man, prone, like all decent men, to doubt, striving to be impartial, finding, in the end, with his heart.

'That Tarlin has always been a troublemaker, sir. Lucky he's flat on his back and in the sick bay, and can't make trouble now. But he's already sending messages out to his friends and of course we can't stop him having visitors. He thinks he was cheated. He thinks he has been savagely injured by a foul blow.'

'In a way he's quite right. Does he think his own boxing above reproach?'

'He's contrived a new picture of it all, sir. His head was slightly tilted forward, he says, not in a butting position at all. Mr Legh, he says, deliberately reached too far to deliver that rabbit punch.'

'How does he explain that he was parallel to the ground as he fell?'

'He just says that a punch from behind would make a man fall flat on his face in the way he did.'

'And all his cronies believe him?'

'Never mind, sir. We'll drop him at the military hospital at Mombasa. It'll be a long time before he appears again. He'll soon be forgotten.'

'Not on this ship. Can't we keep people away from him?'

'He's been very nastily hurt, sir, however it all came about and by the fault of whomsoever. You would not grudge him a few friends for his comfort – trouble-stirrer as he is?'

'I suppose not. Can you make sure that the men do not…get over-excited – when Mr Legh appears in the ring tomorrow evening?'

'Mr Legh, as you know, sir, is to fight Corporal Lendrick. Corporal Lendrick is a graceful boxer and a fair man…in every way. Corporal Lendrick will commit no fouls. There must be none coming from Mr Legh, for all his inexperience.'

'I realise that. All I ask is that the audience shall give him a proper chance, let him start again from scratch.'

'I'll do my best, sir.'

'Thank you, RSM.'

The RSM had always loved his men and served them well, and they knew it. When he put it about that Legh was a tyro who had meant no harm to Tarlin, and that he was to be given a straight chance to re-establish himself as a sportsman and a gentleman, his word was regarded. Even the Tarlin faction was prepared to watch and wait, uneasily aware that their principal's case was not as clean as he urged.

The only people who misbehaved when Legh stepped into the ring to fight Corporal Lendrick were the two senior wives, who had again come to watch with Colonel Cuth. They cackled and jabbered, these respectable upper-middle-class women, as I knew they would if they were allowed to come. I had asked Malcolm to ask the Colonel not to bring them; surely they had been conspicuous enough for their noisy antics on the occasion of Legh's first fight, I said; let them not come again. Malcolm had agreed and made a hint to the Colonel, which had been ill received. They were merely interested, the Colonel had told Malcolm, very interested; surely nobody could object to that. Clearly their husbands were embarrassed, I thought now; otherwise they too would have come. But there was no helping the matter at this stage. Richard Legh and Corporal Lendrick sat in their corners; the two women squawked, the bell rang, the boxers came out and shook hands. The women made elaborate shushing noises and gestured at each other like a Punch and Judy show, then turned their eyes to devour gaunt, gangling Richard and beautiful Lendrick, who was as perfect as a fifth-century statue of Hermes, except for a very slightly snub nose.

If anyone had been expecting the kind of action we'd had in the Legh – Tarlin encounter, then he was to be disappointed. Connoisseurs of human oddity, however, had a banquet. Neither man even attempted to hit the other. They sparred gently round the ring, exchanging little pats on each other's gloves, sometimes feinting, to no purpose, sometimes even aiming a blow, but a blow that always stopped short or landed harmlessly on the other's open glove, which was waiting to receive it long before it arrived.

At the end of the round, the Colonel rose from his place and beckoned me to an empty corner of the ring.

'They're not trying, either of them,' he said. 'They're playing with each other. It's a disgrace.'

'Legh is nervous, sir. You will remember he injured Tarlin very seriously in his last bout.'

'Looks like a put-up job to me. I want to see some proper boxing; tell them.'

So I went first to Legh.

'The Colonel thinks you're not in earnest.'

'He's right. How could I strike a face as beautiful as that?'

Then I went to Lendrick.

'The CO thinks you're playing pit-a-pat.'

'It's clear that Mr Legh is not going to hit me, sir. How can I hit him?'

'Hit him once – over the eye,' I said.

'Sir?'

'Please do as I ask.'

The bell rang for the second round. The wives uncrossed their legs, leant forward and splayed. Lendrick, a good boxer, hit Legh sharply above the left eye.

'That's better,' the Colonel observed aloud, breaking the rule of silence.

'Stop,' I called.

Both boxers stood back. I examined Legh's left eye and made a sign to the doctor. He too examined Legh's eye.

'A gash,' I said. 'Skin broken. Not bleeding yet.'

All this quite loudly, for the Colonel to hear.

'Slow bleeding,' said Wosking. 'It'll start gushing if it's hit again. 'I'd advise you to stop the thing.'

The MO left the ring.

'Mr Legh retires with injuries to the eye,' I announced. 'Corporal Lendrick is the winner.'

Legh and Lendrick shook hands and smiled at each other. One of the women let out her breath with a slight but unmistakable hiss. Never mind her, I thought: thank God we've got Richard out of this quite plausibly and without more trouble.

'And now about that farce with Legh and Lendrick,' the Colonel said. 'I'll admit you covered up quite neatly for them. But why wouldn't they box properly?'

'I told you at the time, sir. Legh was nervous because he'd hurt Tarlin so badly.'

'Accident.'

'Accident or no, he didn't want another.'

'You're saying he's soft.'

'Civilised, sir.'

'And Lendrick? He made one proper punch, but did nothing at all for the whole of the first round.'

'Chivalry, sir. He understood Legh's problem and would not take advantage.'

'That's not how wars are won. We are going to a war, you know.'

Malcolm, sitting behind the CO, raised the fingers of one hand very slightly. 'Don't get into a quarrel about *that*,' the gesture said.

'What jobs do they do, Legh and Lendrick?' said the CO over his shoulder to Malcolm.

'Lendrick is in the bugle platoon, sir. Routine administrative duties when not playing with the bugles or the band.'

'And Legh?'

'Liaison, sir. Or so I thought. He teaches Swahili, as you know.'

'He's not going to liaise with blacks, is he? Only with their white officers.'

'Correct, sir.'

'Then what has teaching Swahili to do with his possible appointment as liaison officer?'

'Nothing in particular, sir. But it does indicate a certain dexterity of mind' – for a second Malcolm's face was impish – 'a quality somewhat rare among your officers.'

'What else makes him suitable?'

'He has the manners of a gentleman, and is lucid and accurate in his speech. He will do us credit with other regiments.'

'He is also,' said the Colonel, 'mealy-mouthed and longwinded. You are obviously in his favour, Raven. But would you not admit that he is mealy-mouthed and verbose?'

'He tries to see things from every possible point of view, sir. This makes for complication and qualification.'

'And his unction? His air of moral self-congratulation?'

'The fault of his college, sir. Corpus Christi, Oxford. A very high-minded and sanctimonious institution.'

God knows why I should have dragged Corpus Christi into it. No reason at all, of course. I just spoke off the top of my head.

'Corpus Christi, Oxford?' said the CO. 'My grandfather's college. He was a fine man and a dedicated – and distinguished – Schoolmaster.'

This was new to me and, to judge from his face, to Malcolm.

'He too,' said Colonel Smith, 'tended to be what you call sanctimonious. But that was not the only attribute he brought away from Corpus Christi. There were honour and truth, to name two more. I think I must get to know Mr Legh rather better. Mark him down as intelligence officer, Malcolm, for the time being. That way he'll be in battalion HQ and always available for liaison if needed. Thank you, Simon,' the CO said, using my Christian name for the first time, 'I'm very glad to know that Richard Legh was at Corpus Christi.'

'So all's well that ends well,' I said to Malcolm.

'No, it's not. Just for a start…why do you think Colonel Cuth didn't know that Richard Legh was at Corpus – before you told him?'

'Colonel Cuth is not interested in universities in the usual way. He heard Richard was from Oxford and that was enough – more than enough, it seemed at the time. He's the kind of man – Colonel Cuth – who's more interested in people's schools than their colleges.'

'More or less right. But it *was*, of course, recorded in Richard's file when he arrived…some time before Colonel Cuth. So far, then, Colonel Cuth has not got round to the personal files of very junior officers – he's had enough to read through without that. Sooner or later – much sooner, now that he's taking this sudden interest – he's going to read Richard's file, the one that came with him from OCTU, and what do you think he is going to find?'

'It can't be anything very dreadful.'

'He's going to find that Richard's father and mother were prominent members of the Peace Pledge Union in the Thirties. They actually campaigned against the waging of the 39-45 war and for a time they were put in a detention camp – from 1941 to 1943.'

'But so long as none of this was concealed when Richard joined the army, or when he was later interviewed by the Colonel of the regiment, there is nothing to be said about it.'

'Colonel Cuth won't like it.'

'He didn't like Richard before. Now, it seems, he does. When he finds out about his parents, perhaps he won't. So sodding what?'

'Because of *your* remark about Corpus,' said Malcolm, 'Richard Legh is to be intelligence officer. What happens to him when the Colonel reads that file?'

'If Cuth has got any sense at all, he keeps him as intelligence officer. The point about Richard is that he believes, on intellectual grounds, in obedience to the state and those in authority under it.'

'The Colonel believes in heredity. He believes his grandparents and his parents made him what he is. Because his grandfather was at Corpus, Corpus is a good thing (no matter that Cuth distrusts graduates as a rule) and because Richard was at Corpus, Richard becomes a good thing despite having displeased the Colonel till now. But when Cuth finds out that Richard's father and mother were pacifists, he will cease to trust him (heredity again). So either he will sack Richard from the post of IO, which will be a very bad thing for confidence and discipline in the battalion as a whole, or he will keep Richard as IO but continue to mistrust him, which will be a very bad thing for the Colonel's work and Richard's, and for the efficiency of battalion HQ.

'And what will make it all one hundred times worse,' continued Malcolm, 'is that gallant Colonel Cuth thinks that we are riding to war, when we are going to Kenya only in an administrative role, to help clean things up. What is even worse is that our arrival is going to coincide with the last remotely warlike operation that will be staged – i.e. the bombing of the Aberdare Forest – and this, although it is only intended to bring the Mau Mau out of the forest for beneficent detention, will confirm Cuth in thinking we are at war and in behaving accordingly. Last and worst of all is the apparent determination of the GOC-in-C to send us into the forest to provide ambushes to net the terrorists before we have had any training in any jungle role whatever. What we now need, therefore, like we need an outbreak of bubonic plague, is an internal crisis in battalion HQ which brings Cuth into unfounded and emotional mistrust of his intelligence officer.'

'Lose the file. Make out a temporary one which does not go into detail about Richard's parents.'

'Unfortunately my ORQMS is neither as biddable nor as versatile as the doctor's Flossie. Oh, for more Flossies in this world,' Malcolm wailed. 'But I have removed Richard's file from the orderly room for "Adjutant's perusal" and I think I can keep it away from Cuth for a very long time – if only he doesn't call for it before we reach Mombasa. Once we're there he's going to be much too busy to start fussing about personal files.'

When we reached Mombasa, we were met by the GOC-in-C, who took Colonel Cuth in his helicopter to Nairobi, thus leaving Malcolm and the second-in-command of the battalion (an amiable and bibulous cricketer, who did precisely what Malcolm told him) to bring the rest of us up by train.

'Thank God,' said Malcolm disloyally, 'that the General has taken You Know Who. I think we were in for an obsession about train discipline – sitting to attention in full battle order in case we were attacked. I do hope the General can make Cuth understand that all that is over. The truth is, Cuth enjoys that sort of thing so much. He's the kind of man who reads *Boys' Own* until he's forty.'

The men travelled third class, in exactly the same way as African Askaris (soldiers): hard seats with haversack rations. Warrant officers and serjeants went second class, with their own egg-and-chippy restaurant. Officers rode first class, with a deluxe restaurant (Portuguese oysters and game).

'It's nice to know,' said O., 'that Kenyans still have a correct social perspective.'

'I'm told,' said our point-to-point rider, 'that flat racing in Nairobi is lively but corrupt and there is quite a good steeplechase course near Naivasha, where they run the Kenya Grand National. This will be the second year they've held it since the Mau Mau rebellion ceased.'

'Ah,' said Malcolm, 'will you please tell that to the Colonel 500 times. "Sir," you must say, "can I have leave to ride in the Kenya Grand National, which has been running again for several years now that the emergency is well and truly over?" I shall see that you get the leave if only you will apply for it often enough. I cannot emphasise too much to you all,' he said, 'that only romantics like Colonel Cuth and a few careerist last ditchers still conceive that there is a war here. I rely on you Richard,' he said to Legh, 'to discountenance any tendency towards belligerence or competition.'

'Competition?'

'Yes. As you know, even now there are occasional circumstances in which the Mau Mau have to be shot. Certain officers, who should know better, keep a tally of killings and circulate their scores. Some of these think that their enthusiasm will be rewarded by promotion. Some of them are just haters of blacks. In either case they are very bad news.'

'In other words,' said O., 'you are counselling us *not* to get on with the job?'

O. was always bating his seniors; one sees why he never became a general or even a brigadier.

'I am counselling you,' said Malcolm through his teeth, 'to be quite sure what the job is before getting on with it.'

'And what form will it take during the forthcoming operation in the Aberdare Forest?'

'We shall be told soon enough,' said Malcolm, and ground his molars.

Once in Nairobi, we settled into a tented camp in the suburbs, near a luxurious country club of which all officers were made honorary members. The men were less fortunate; their canteens were fly-blown and ill provided.

'The sooner we get out of here and into the forest, the better,' said O., as we stood by the barrack square, waiting for nothing to happen. 'It will take just three days more for the men to find out how to get to the brothel area; and then watch out.'

'This operation in the Aberdares may be a blessing in disguise then? Even if we haven't been trained for the jungle.'

'Anything must be better than rotting away in this horrible suburb.'

'We've got the Muthaiga Club.'

'*You and I* have got the Muthaiga Club.'

'And that Swiss restaurant. They somehow get marvellous veal.'

'Such a consolation to Corporal Lendrick and his chums, to know that you're dining off tender veal.'

Our amateur race-rider sauntered up.

'The Colonel's got a new fixation,' he said 'ABCA: The Army Bureau of Current Affairs.'

'Does it still exist?'

'If it doesn't he's going to revive it. All platoon commanders must be prepared to give daily lectures on European and African matters, if possible relating them. Weather, geography, trade, ethnic composition, language; anything except politics.'

'All the platoon commanders,' I gloated. 'That lets me out.'

'No, it doesn't. Officers second-in-command of companies will lecture the personnel of company headquarters.'

'That's the company commanders' job.'

'They're going to be too busy making a recce of their companies' positions for Operation Exlax.'

'Operation *what*?'

'The idea is,' said O., 'that the jungle will be opening its bowels to void all the remaining Mau Mau...into our ambushes.'

'They'd better hurry,' said the jockey, 'or there'll be no ambushes left. Four of my chaps have already reported with clap.'

'They've found their way to the brothels already?'

'The whole place is a brothel. You've only got to take one step out of the camp. That's why we're going to have all this ABCA. The chaps will be set homework in the evenings so that they won't have time to go out.'

'A little training might be a good thing,' said O.

'Unfortunately,' I said, 'they've just withdrawn all our jungle boots. Defective issue, it seems. The new lot was due in this morning, but all that arrived was ping-pong tables.'

'Pingers,' said O., 'just the thing to take their minds off zigzag.'

'There are neither nets, balls nor bats. Just tables.'

'I must be off,' said the point-to-point rider, 'to give my ABCA lecture to my platoon. I've got just the job for today. I'm calling it, "The Manners and Morals of Happy Valley" – about the settlers.'

'The Muthaiga Club has a cricket ground,' I said to O. 'We might get up a match.'

'No kit, old bean. Except for ten pairs of bails.'

My company serjeant-major came up. 'Ten cases of clap for orders, sir,' he said.

'The company commander is going to love that,' I said.

The RSM came up.

'Morning, gentlemen,' he said. 'Preliminary warning. The CO is going to call a curfew. No personnel allowed out of camp after 1800 hours except on duty.'

'Not even for dinner, RSM?'

'*No* personnel, sir, not even for dinner.'

'ABCA,' said O. as the two warrant officers departed, 'was bliss compared with this.'

'We'd better go into Nairobi,' I said, 'to stock up with caviar and stuff.'

'Won't keep long out here.'

'There is a refrigerator in the cookhouse.'

'Not for storing officers' caviar,' said Malcolm, who was looking very regimental in khaki shorts (cut just above the knee) with boots and puttees, and carrying an ebony light infantry cane with a silver knob.

'I'm on my way to commanding officer's orders,' he said, 'where the curfew is to be announced.'

'Why didn't you warn us?'

'I didn't know until a few minutes ago. The idea is that if they're not allowed out the men will pay more attention to their evening homework for their ABCA studies. And you lot will be able to prepare your lectures more carefully.'

Malcolm marched off, swinging his cane parallel to the ground, like a guardsman walking out in Windsor Park before the war.

Richard Legh came up.

'Heard about the curfew?' he said. 'Well, I've arranged to be liaising with other liaisers from all units in the Muthaiga Club every night this week. Duty, you see.'

'For a Corpus Christi man, you're getting very smooth and worldly.'

'I have arranged with the CO that I can take two friends with me every evening to help me liaise. Want to come, boys?'

'Yes,' we said. Richard passed on as if wearing seven-league boots.

'Success has changed him,' said O. 'Three weeks ago he wouldn't have called us "boys" to save his life.'

'Success has improved him,' I said. 'He's no longer a howling prig. And it was kind of him to remember us in his scheme for curfew-dodging. There's many as wouldn't.'

Lieutenant (Doctor) Wosking stumped past.

'There's a medical officers' conference at the Muthaiga Club,' Lieutenant Wosking said, 'every evening for the next fortnight. I'm allowed to take two officers from the battalion to put their problems to the learned doctors assembled. Strictly duty, of course, but we shall adjourn after half an hour for dinner. Any use to you two?'

'Thanks. But we're already fixed up.'

The second-in-command of B Company came up.

'Ah, Simon,' he said. 'There's a special committee of seconds-in-command, to discuss the problems raised for us by Operation Exlax. To last ten days, or until Exlax actually begins. Every evening from 1830 hours.'

'At the Muthaiga Club?'

'No. All the special rooms there are already booked. We've taken the banqueting room in the Swiss restaurant, *pro tem*, but we've got first option on a cancellation at the New Stanley Hotel.'

'Which is the better for dinner,' I said to O., 'the Muthaiga or the New Stanley? Or the Swiss restaurant?'

'The Muthaiga do those giant prawns, flown up iced from the coast. The New Stanley has a good line in snails cooked in Burgundy. But as you yourself say, there's nothing to beat the veal at the Swiss place.'

'What an agonising decision. I'll tell you what,' I said to my brother second-in-command, 'I'm booked for the liaison officers' *soirée*, but I might switch to the second-in-commands' committee in a few days.'

'We'd be honoured, I'm sure.'

The Quartermaster Major, a dour Methodist killjoy, came past.

'I hear the CO has put a spoke in the wheel of pleasure,' he said with relish. 'A curfew from now on.'

'Yes, Q.,' we said demurely. 'Very sensible. We must get on with getting on with the job, must we not?'

'Rotten dinner in the mess last night,' said Malcolm at midmorning break next day.

'Oh yes?'

'Tinned stew. Only the Colonel and me and the QM eating it. Even the padre was out…at a prayer meeting in the Muthaiga Club.'

'You know how important all this liaison and…er…er…the rest of it is?' said O. 'They say the GOC-in-C is tremendously in favour of it.'

'There will have to be a rota,' said Malcolm. 'One volunteer every evening to keep the Colonel company.'

'He's got the QM.'

'The QM has gone on a fortnight's course, on the maintenance of stores in the tropics.'

'I'll tell you what,' O. said. 'We'll all chip in with five bob an evening and draw lots. The lucky man wins about ten quid and gets the Colonel for dinner.'

'He might smell a rat fairly soon,' I said.

'He's already smelling it,' said Malcolm.

'Another suggestion,' said O. 'Send him off to inspect the company commanders who are inspecting their positions for Exlax. All four rifle companies are on the perimeter of the forest covering the arc from Fort Hall to Naivasha. It'll take him some days to move round that lot.'

'Then there'd be no officers in camp at night at all.'

'Yes there would,' said O., 'the orderly officer. Why didn't we think of that before? Where was he last night, by the way?'

'I agreed to stand in for him,' said Malcolm, 'but it's rather *infra dig* and I shan't do it again.'

'The Muthaiga is not good for you,' said O. to Malcolm. 'You're altogether too plump and sweaty already. You'd do yourself a good turn by having a few more nights in the mess with the Colonel and tinned stew.'

'Thank you. I feel as if I were developing duodenal ulcers. That being the case, I must have a lot of soothing cream in my food. The only place I shall get that will be in the Muthaiga Club. So be it – and the orderly officer, as you very sensibly suggest, can dine in every night, with or without the CO. I wish to God they'd give the order to take up positions for Exlax.'

'On the boat you said you were dreading it.'

'I was. But not so much as I am now dreading the Brigadier's reaction to today's VD returns: we have the worst record of any battalion ever to have been in Kenya.'

'Oh dear. Obviously we need even more ABCA... Have they sent the new jungle boots yet?'

'No. A consignment of dartboards without any darts.'

'Clearly,' said O., 'in the absence of other entertainments for the troops, VD is the only alternative to having a mutiny. So let's settle for VD. But if you're really bothered, can't the padre do anything?'

'He is at least clean,' I ventured.

That evening, Richard Legh and I walked back together after the liaison officers' jamboree at the Muthaiga Club. (O. had decided to spend the night there, in anticipation of crapula.)

'As intelligence officer of this battalion,' said Richard, 'I must read all official handouts and computations. As liaison officer among others of that ilk I discover just what rubbish the handouts and computations are. Take these ambushes we are going to provide for Exlax. As you know, the policy is that any Mau Mau who come out of the Aberdare Forest should be captured, not killed. All very proper and humane. There is just one teeny weeny snag, as Wigmore of the rifles was pointing out this evening. As a matter of statistics most of the Mau Mau are diseased. Each group of them is allotted a couple of whores from Nairobi, who are smuggled into their area – and then pox the lot.'

'Just like our battalion,' I said.

'You've put your finger on the problem. There is only a certain amount of penicillin available to the army and for other official purposes. What with our own patients – and though our battalion may be worst, the others are neck and neck for close second – and what with the supplies that are "lost" – i.e. sold to the madams and the black market – there is not very much left over for Mau Mau captives. Now, if the army captures as many live Mau Mau during Exlax as theory declares possible and if they are all sent to internment camps, there simply will not be enough penicillin in the whole of Kenya to cure a quarter of them.'

'Send for more penicillin.'

'Wigmore says that such a request would give the show away. There'd be a tremendous row about the amount needed by the army and somebody would prod his pointed nose into the scandal of the supplies that have gone missing. Bad trouble for everybody – not just the bootleggers.'

'So what are we going to do? Shoot the Mau Mau as they come out of the jungle instead of capturing them?'

'Either that, or have thousands of them sitting round in internment camps slowly decaying at the taxpayers' expense.'

'I wonder they're going to have the operation at all,' I said.

'They can't cancel it, because too many distinguished people are coming out to watch.'

'There won't be anything to watch. You can't have distinguished spectators hanging around with the ambushes. The marquees for their meals would give the game away. What else is there for them to see?'

'Bombers taking off. Guns firing. Anyway, that's GHQ's business. To revert to ours. The official instruction will still be to capture the Mau Mau, but in the case of inexperienced troops, like our own, who cannot be expected to handle live and hostile blacks, the order will be to shoot when in doubt – i.e., unless the enemy comes forward peacefully and gives himself up immediately.'

'And who will take the responsibility for this order? The official policy is capture and arrest, but in practice our boys are to be told to shoot. At which…descending stage in the hierarchy…is the doctrine to be subtly transformed? And what line are these pestering magistrates going to take?'

Richard and I waited by the barrier at the camp entrance. We were challenged ('Get you the sons your fathers got') and gave the answer, 'And God will save the Queen'. A sullen lance-corporal lifted the barrier, while a dopey sentry wrongly presented arms, on the off-chance we were somebody more important.

'That your idea?' I said. 'Housman for the password?'

'It seemed appropriate. The poet of Shropshire and Hereford.'

'I wonder what he would have made of all this?

> "The files move slowly past," ' Richard quoted,
> ' "Towards the hollow;
> The bugles sound again;
> The soldiers follow."

That says it all in the end.'*

'What it does not say,' I said, 'is that they may be charged with murder by some malign little pinko prick with a temporary magistracy, if they panic and shoot in their own protection.'

---

* It was only many years later that I realised that Richard Legh was misquoting or improvising on this – to me at least – memorable occasion. In fact there is a Housman poem that ends, 'The soldiers follow'; but the rest of Richard's quotation is corrupt.

'Oh no,' said Richard. 'Wigmore has told me what to do. As intelligence officer, I shall be first on the scene after any killing, and I have a number of captured Mau Mau weapons, supplied by Wigmore and others, with which to rig the tableau if necessary. Remember, proven self-defence is an absolute get-out in this game, even with pinko magistrates umpiring. And now you're going to ask what they'd say about *that* in Corpus Christi, Oxford?'

'I was rather wondering.'

'My parents were pacifists, you know.'

'So I believe.'

'Friends of Aldous Huxley and Gerald Heard. They died not long after the war. They left some reputation behind them and this was one of the reasons why Corpus Christi was happy to accept me.'

'Ironic. The Colonel first took to you because his grandfather was at Corpus. And now we learn that Corpus welcomed you for your pacifist connections.'

'But the point I wish to make is that neither my parents nor the high-minded dons of Corpus understood a necessity which they had never been required to face. Plato, echoed by Marcus Aurelius, tells us that it is one's duty to stay at one's post until one is ordered to retire or killed by the enemy; that it is one's duty to carry out one's orders but also to survive if possible. If you do not meet violence with violence, very often you cannot survive.'

'But we were talking about rigging the truth in order to avoid charges of murder.'

'In order to help others avoid charges of murder. My conscience is quite clear, Simon. Our soldiers are very young and frightened men far from home and far from Jerusalem. They are going to be pitched into the jungle without training or preparation and told to stop any black man that tries to come out of it. They must therefore be given absolutely clear orders and be defended by us if they get into trouble while obeying them. So that it is, after all, just as well that Colonel Cuthbert thinks this is a war. He is going to address each platoon in the next few days, and tell them that it is their right and their duty, if in any doubt whatever, to fire on any Mau Mau that come their way.'

'Thus to the great but concealed joy of the authorities diminishing the numbers that require penicillin.'

'There is so much hypocrisy going about that it is a pleasure to work with Colonel Cuth Smith. It's a pity about these obsessive hankerings of his, but if it hadn't been for them I don't suppose I'd have come to his attention. In most matters he is admirably honest and direct: they need a breath of him to blow through the senior common room in Corpus Christi.'

One week later, all our companies were in position between Fort Hall and Naivasha. Each company would send into the forest, and then from time to time relieve, eight ambushes of five men. The distances between the company encampment and the ambush positions would vary from a mile to a mile and a half, a march just tolerable in the men's new and badly fitting jungle boots.

Battalion field headquarters was in a farmhouse about twenty miles from Fort Hall, a few hundred yards from the main road, or rather the main track, that led from Fort Hall along the edge of the forest to the escarpment. Hardly had Cuth arrived there with Malcolm as Adjutant, Richard Legh as intelligence (liaison) officer, the RSM and other attendant personnel, when there was a very annoying scene.

The settler who owned the farmhouse did not live in it (he had several more) but nevertheless conceived that his ownership gave him the right to enter at will and hobnob with Colonel Cuthbert. By way of initial introduction, he arrived drunk and demanding more drink. He was told that the field HQ mess was not yet established; if he would care to come back tomorrow evening… Bugger tomorrow evening, he wanted a drink and don't try to fob him off or he'd have the battalion HQ evicted from his property.

Since Richard was the youngest and (he supposed) the most vulnerable officer present, he concentrated his demands and his threats on him. Finally Richard simply ordered him to go, was threatened with violence, called in a corporal and two men of the regimental police, and instructed them to lock the settler in an outhouse until he was sober…unless he consented to leave at once. The settler went roaring off in his Land Rover, toppled off the track a few miles down it and broke his neck.

This meant that Richard, who had seen him off in every sense and was the last person (together with the regimental policemen) to see him alive, had to answer a number of questions from the Kenya police. They settled into the farmhouse to make a real meal of it; among other things, they demanded to see Richard's army documents, were taken down by Malcolm to Nairobi, where Richard's file now was (having long since been replaced by Malcolm in its correct place in the orderly room cabinets), and were invited to inspect it. Now, although the regular Kenya police were not a bad lot, the temporary officers, who had been recruited for the emergency, were muck…and, since they knew that their employment was about to end as the emergency finally dwindled to nothing, poisonous muck for ill measure. Although it had nothing to do with the case in hand, they became hostile and suspicious on learning that Richard was an Oxford graduate, and additionally so when they had read what the records said of his parents. The line they began to take was that Richard had been high-handed and inhospitable to the settler, had forcibly expelled him from his own territory, well knowing that he was in no fit state to drive, and had thus indirectly but culpably brought about a fatal accident. They attempted to arrest Richard on trumped-up charges of manslaughter, were themselves arrested for threatening a commissioned officer of Her Majesty while he was performing his duties on active service and were taken away to the police station at Fort Hall, where the superintendent, an old-time police officer, suspended and confined them, and ultimately had them dismissed. But in the course of all this Colonel Cuth called for the file that had provoked their hostility and zeal, and now discovered that his intelligence (liaison) officer was the son of militant pacifists.

As Malcolm had apprehended, Cuth did not like it at all. All his former prejudice against Richard was now renewed; his earlier enthusiasm for the products of Corpus Christi was most damnably vitiated by his recalling that that 'fine man', his grandfather, had intervened in some quarrel between the Senate House of Oxford and the War Office, a quarrel to do with the status of officers sent by the War Office to study the natural sciences. Since such officers were normally mature men, the War Office requested that they should not be subjected to the puerile regulations then imposed on ordinary commoners but should be invited to dine at High Table and, in general, treated as gentlemen commoners. When informed that the rank of gentleman commoner no longer existed, the War Office suggested a special grade, carrying special privileges, for all officers of more than five years' service, a suggestion that was peremptorily rejected. Cuth now remembered that his grandfather had been prominent among the anti-military group in this fracas, and his former suspicions of Richard were revived and magnified.

'I have persuaded the Colonel to keep him on as IO until this operation is over,' said Malcolm, while pausing one afternoon at my company encampment. 'Richard has studied the territory with great care, and it would be both unfair and injurious to send him packing just as the circus is coming to town.'

'And when Operation Exlax is over?'

'We shall see. If only it hadn't been for those accursed brutes of temporary policemen, I think I could have kept that file away from Cuth forever.'

'He must see that Richard is still the same man he was getting on so well with?'

'Yes. The same man, but now flawed with an hereditary infirmity, latent at the moment, but which may at any second start discharging the pus of disaffection.'

'He thinks that Richard may turn on him and denounce the army and all its works?'

'That kind of a thing,' Malcolm said.

A few days later, Richard himself appeared and told the following story:

'The bombardment was stiffened up a bit a short while after the operation began, but nothing much came out of the jungle except a pregnant cow-elephant and no Mau Mau at all. The Colonel became very restless.

' "The boys in the ambushes will be getting pretty bored," he said, "bored and damp. How can we encourage them?"

"We can't," I said. "Ambushing is a thankless task. You have to stay still, without food or rest or movement, for hours on end. If you want to pee, you have to piddle where you sit." I turned from my desk to the Colonel. "I've been talking, sir, to Captain Kitson of the rifles. You know he used to specialise, before the emergency was over, in cloak and dagger operations?"

' "And so?" said the Colonel peevishly.

"Kitson says that one of our handicaps in the jungle was that we smelt too clean. If we'd made the men go without baths and without shaving, we'd have had a better chance. As it was…the hygienic smell of the white men radiated hundreds of yards before and behind them. We'd have done much better, Kitson says, to stink like the Mau Mau."

' "And so?" the Colonel said again.

' "Have I your permission, sir, to request company commanders to send out their ambushes unwashed? So that they can't give themselves away by their cleanliness?"

' "And what would that do for morale?" said a company commander, who had dropped in on battalion HQ to make a nil return.

' "If it were explained to the men, they would understand why they were doing it and, however repugnant they found it," I said, "they would do it without complaint."

'But the CO wasn't listening.

' "I've got an idea," he said. "Where's Malcolm?"

' "He had to go to Nairobi, sir. With the second-in-command. Corporal Lendrick's court martial, if you remember."

'For Lendrick, as you may have heard, caught the first pox in the bugle platoon since we came to Kenya.

' "In the middle of a major operation," the Colonel said, "they have to waste time and energy on court martials."

' "Courts martial," I corrected, stupidly and officiously, doing nothing to mend matters.

' "Since Malcolm isn't here," said the CO with distaste, "you had better come with me. You and the RSM," he called.

' "Sir?"

' "We are going to go round some of the ambushes, to cheer the boys up and put them on their mettle, now that the bombardment is being stepped up."

' "We are going where, sir?"

' "Round some of the ambushes. Your company is the nearest," he said to the company commander who was there. "You can guide us out to your ambushes."

'The Company Commander [Richard told us now] opened his mouth and shut it.

' "We don't need any guides," I told the Colonel. "I have an exact chart of all ambushes. In any case, sir, it is impossible that we should go to them."

' "Oh? Why? Oblige us with your superior wisdom."

' "Ambushes are not to be disturbed, sir. It gives away the position. Besides...as I said just now, they are meant to sit and wait. They are also meant…to apprehend or to shoot anyone who approaches them."

' "They'll recognise us," said the CO.

' "With the greatest respect, sir," said the RSM, "I think that Mr Legh may be right. It is difficult to recognise people through thick forest."

' "Mr Legh," said the company commander, "is an Oxford man. He likes to keep his hands nice and clean. He doesn't want to go into the horrid jungle."

' "I didn't notice, Major Lambert," said I, "that you were any too forward in the matter yourself. However, I shall be happy to accompany the commanding officer if that is what he wishes. But I should be rather happier if he would wait for the return and advice of his Adjutant."

' "I respectfully agree, gentlemen," said the RSM.

' "You are against this, Legh." the Colonel said.

' "I am, sir."

' "I might have known you would be. I've been expecting something of the kind for days." And to the RSM, "We shall be needing a party of four askaris★ to accompany us. To assist us if we meet any of the enemy."

' "We have the bugle platoon here, sir. Some of them – '

' " – No, RSM. We need Africans. They understand the jungle better than we do. How soon can you collect them?"

'As you know [Richard told us at my company encampment] O. is in charge of the Africans. I prayed he would back me up and help stop this idiocy. But when the RSM and I came to their quarters, O. wasn't there. He was away in Naivasha, consulting with officers of the African rifles about the best methods of handling black soldiers. There was only an African serjeant there, who at once picked and paraded a detail of his men.'

'Oh Richard. What happened next?'

★ Loyal black troops.

'What happened next was that the company commander who had been on a visit to battalion HQ slunk away when nobody was looking. The CO's servant appeared with a sack of goods – Coca-Cola, chocolate, NAAFI wodges [cakes or buns].

' "Father Christmas," the CO joked. "You carry the sack, Legh. You're the junior man."

'The RSM cleared his throat.

' "Senior warrant officers don't carry sacks," said the CO. "There's no reason why very junior National Service officers shouldn't."

' "The Africans are outside, sir. Perhaps one of them – '

' "The Africans have their own duties. Among them to sniff out possible danger from the Mau Mau." And to his servant, ' "Give the sack to Mr Legh."

'So off we went [Richard told us], two Africans in the lead, to spot rhino or buffalo, and Africans also in the rear. Colonel Cuth led the whites; the RSM was still, for some reason, carrying his pace stick; and I carried the sack of goodies to cheer up the ambushes and a map. I know what I'll do, I thought. I'll guide them between two of the ambushes – make us miss them all.

' "I'd better get up front, sir," I said, "in order to direct us."

' "No need, sir," said the good old RSM, too thick to see what I was at. "Some of these Africans went out when the ambushes was put into position. They know exactly which way to go."

'And so we wagged along through the forest…until a rifle cracked to front right of us, and the Colonel staggered and fell. One of the ambush told me afterwards that he had fired at a black face. Not one of the blacks was scratched. Our rifleman had missed the Africans and shot the Colonel. Who shall say that justice was not done?

'One of the Africans in the rear was fitted with an RT set. The RSM tried to reach HQ. I attended to Cuth. It seemed more sensible to let him lie, from what little First Aid I knew, rather than to prop him up. Always leave them where they are until the doctor comes, I'd been told. So I left the Colonel where he was on the ground. I wondered what to do about his wound – wherever it was. I could see the blood in his throat when he spoke.

' "What happened?" he said.

' "You've been shot, sir."

' "You were right, Richard, weren't you? One shouldn't disturb an ambush. What was I thinking of?"

' "Don't talk, sir, please don't talk. The RSM is sending for the MO."

' "He will need a guide. It will take time."

' "*Don't talk, sir.*"

' "Prop me up."

' "It is better you lie flat."

' "I'm choking, Richard."

'So I propped him up. Although a little blood spilled from his mouth, he seemed better for a while. I held my handkerchief against the wound which, I now saw, was high in his chest.

' "The doctor is on his way, sir," said the RSM. "He says we're not to move the Colonel at all."

' "Mr Legh has his orders," said the CO. "He is to prop me up."

'The RSM turned away and muttered, "God have mercy. Christ have mercy. God have mercy. What a fuck-up."

' "Come," said Colonel Cuth. "I hope we need not talk of God just yet."

' "Please, my Colonel, don't talk."

"There is something that must be said. Tell the boys from the ambush to come here."

'The RSM fetched the five men of the ambush.

' "It wasn't your fault," the Colonel said to them. "Never, in all your lives, feel guilty. You were doing your duty and did it well. *It wasn't your fault.* Now resume your positions."

'He seemed to faint then and when the MO came, three-quarters of an hour later, he was dead. I don't know how long he had been dead. He said nothing more after he'd spoken to the men of the ambush. A good death. I thought of Falstaff babbling of green fields. I don't know why. Cuth didn't babble at all, and there was never a man less like Falstaff. I suppose...green fields seemed right for him. Cuthbert, the country boy. The Shropshire lad.'

SIMON RAVEN

MORNING STAR

This first volume in Simon Raven's *First-Born of Egypt* saga opens with the christening of the Marquess Canteloupe's son and heir, Sarum of Old Sarum. The ceremony, attended by the godparents and the real father, Fielding Gray, is not without drama.

The christening introduces a bizarre cast of eccentric characters and complicated relationships. In *Morning Star* we meet the brilliant but troublesome teenager Marius Stern. Marius' increasingly outrageous behaviour has him constantly on the verge of expulsion from prep school. When his parents are kidnapped, apparently without reason, events take a turn for the worse.

THE FACE OF THE WATERS

This is the second volume of Simon Raven's *First-Born of Egypt* series. Marius Stern, the wayward son of Gregory Stern, has survived earlier escapades and is safely back at prep school – assisted by his father's generous contribution to the school's new shooting-range. Fielding Gray and Jeremy Morrison are returning home via Venice, where they encounter the friar, Piero, an ex-male whore and a figure from a shared but distant past.

Back in England, at the Wiltshire family home, Lord Canteloupe is restless. He finds his calm disturbed by events: the arrival of Piero; Jeremy's father's threat to saddle his son with the responsibility of the family estate; and the dramatic resistance of Gregory Stern to attempted blackmail.

SIMON RAVEN

BEFORE THE COCK CROW

This is the third volume in Simon Raven's *First-Born of Egypt* saga. The story opens with Lord Canteloupe's strange toast to 'absent friends'. His wife Baby has recently died and Canteloupe has been left her retarded son, Lord Sarum of Old Sarum. This child is not his, but has been conceived by Major Fielding Gray. In Italy there is an illegitimate child with a legitimate claim to the estate, whom Canteloupe wants silenced.

NEW SEED FOR OLD

The fourth in the *First-Born of Egypt* series has Lord Canteloupe wanting a satisfactory heir so that his dynasty may continue. Unfortunately, Lord Canteloupe is impotent and his existing heir, little Tully Sarum, is not of sound mind.

His wife Theodosia is prepared to do her duty when a suitable partner is found. Finding the man and the occasion proves somewhat tricky however, and it is not until Lord Canteloupe goes up to Lord's for the first match of the season that progress is made.

SIMON RAVEN

BLOOD OF MY BONE

In this fifth volume of Simon Raven's *First-Born of Egypt* series, the death of the Provost of a large school is a catalyst for a series of disgraceful doings in the continuing saga of the Canteloupes and their circle.

Marius, under-age father of the new Lady Canteloupe's dutifully produced heir to the family estate, is warned against the malign influence of Raisley Conyngham. Classics teacher at his school, Conyngham is well aware of the sway he has over Marius, who has already revealed himself a keen student of 'the refinements of hell'. With fate intervening, the stage is set for another deliciously wicked instalment.

IN THE IMAGE OF GOD

The sixth in the *First-Born of Egypt* series sees Raisley Conyngham, Classics teacher at a large school, exert a powerful influence over Marius Stern. His young pupil, however, is no defenceless victim.

Marius has a ruthless streak and an ability to sidestep tests and traps that are laid for him. Which is just as well because everybody is after something from him…

OTHER TITLES BY SIMON RAVEN AVAILABLE DIRECT
FROM HOUSE OF STRATUS

Quantity		£	$(US)	$(CAN)	€
☐	BEFORE THE COCK CROW	7.99	12.99	17.49	13.00
☐	BLOOD OF MY BONE	7.99	12.99	17.49	13.00
☐	BROTHER CAIN	7.99	12.99	17.49	13.00
☐	CLOSE OF PLAY	7.99	12.99	17.49	13.00
☐	DOCTORS WEAR SCARLET	7.99	12.99	17.49	13.00
☐	THE FACE OF THE WATERS	7.99	12.99	17.49	13.00
☐	THE FORTUNES OF FINGEL	7.99	12.99	17.49	13.00
☐	IN THE IMAGE OF GOD	7.99	12.99	17.49	13.00
☐	AN INCH OF FORTUNE	7.99	12.99	17.49	13.00
☐	MORNING STAR	7.99	12.99	17.49	13.00
☐	NEW SEED FOR OLD	7.99	12.99	17.49	13.00
☐	THE ROSES OF PICARDIE	7.99	12.99	17.49	13.00
☐	SEPTEMBER CASTLE	7.99	12.99	17.49	13.00
☐	SHADOWS ON THE GRASS	7.99	12.99	17.49	13.00
☐	THE TROUBADOUR	7.99	12.99	17.49	13.00

ALL HOUSE OF STRATUS BOOKS ARE AVAILABLE FROM GOOD BOOKSHOPS
OR DIRECT FROM THE PUBLISHER:

Internet: www.houseofstratus.com including author interviews, reviews, features.

Email: sales@houseofstratus.com please quote author, title and credit card details.

Hotline: UK ONLY: 0800 169 1780, please quote author, title and credit card details.
INTERNATIONAL: +44 (0) 20 7494 6400, please quote author, title and credit card details.

Send to: House of Stratus Sales Department
24c Old Burlington Street
London
W1X 1RL
UK

Please allow for postage costs charged per order plus an amount per book as set out in the tables below:

	£(Sterling)	$(US)	$(CAN)	€(Euros)
Cost per order				
UK	2.00	3.00	4.50	3.30
Europe	3.00	4.50	6.75	5.00
North America	3.00	4.50	6.75	5.00
Rest of World	3.00	4.50	6.75	5.00
Additional cost per book				
UK	0.50	0.75	1.15	0.85
Europe	1.00	1.50	2.30	1.70
North America	2.00	3.00	4.60	3.40
Rest of World	2.50	3.75	5.75	4.25

PLEASE SEND CHEQUE, POSTAL ORDER (STERLING ONLY), EUROCHEQUE, OR INTERNATIONAL MONEY ORDER (PLEASE CIRCLE METHOD OF PAYMENT YOU WISH TO USE)
MAKE PAYABLE TO: STRATUS HOLDINGS plc

Cost of book(s): _____ Example: 3 x books at £6.99 each: £20.97

Cost of order: _____ Example: £2.00 (Delivery to UK address)

Additional cost per book: _____ Example: 3 x £0.50: £1.50

Order total including postage: _____ Example: £24.47

Please tick currency you wish to use and add total amount of order:

☐ £ (Sterling)   ☐ $ (US)   ☐ $ (CAN)   ☐ € (EUROS)

VISA, MASTERCARD, SWITCH, AMEX, SOLO, JCB:

☐☐☐☐☐☐☐☐☐☐☐☐☐☐☐☐☐☐☐

Issue number (Switch only):

☐☐☐

Start Date: **Expiry Date:**

☐☐/☐☐   ☐☐/☐☐

Signature: _____

NAME: _____

ADDRESS: _____

_____

POSTCODE: _____

Please allow 28 days for delivery.

Prices subject to change without notice.
Please tick box if you do not wish to receive any additional information. ☐

House of Stratus publishes many other titles in this genre; please check our website (**www.houseofstratus.com**) for more details.